Len Jenkin is a writer who lives and works in New York City. He has written, for the past few years, mostly for the stage, television, and film. *New Jerusalem* marks his return to fiction. His plays include *Limbo Tales*, *Dark Ride*, *My Uncle Sam*, and *American Notes*. His work for the stage has been produced often in theatres in the United States, and twice in London. He is the recipient of National Endowment for the Arts awards, three OBIE awards in the theatre, and Rockefeller and Guggenheim fellowships. Mr. Jenkin is currently at work on a new novel.

LEN JENKIN

New Jerusalem

PALADIN
GRAFTON BOOKS

A Division of the Collins Publishing Group

LONDON GLASGOW
TORONTO SYDNEY AUCKLAND

Paladin
Grafton Books
A Division of the Collins Publishing Group
8 Grafton Street, London W1X 3LA

A Paladin UK Paperback Original 1989

This edition first published in the United
States of America by Sun & Moon Press 1986

Copyright © Len Jenkin 1986

ISBN 0-586-08727-3

Printed and bound in Great Britain by
Collins, Glasgow

Set in Times

for my father

THE NEWSWATCH
NEVER STOPS

Why seek ye the living among the dead?
—*Luke, 24, 5*

I am your reporter, the best, the last, laying it out on the live wire. Current events, pole to pole. You've got ears. Hear me. This story of mine is loud enough to wake the dead, and cure warts. Say it over in your sleep.

I attended a college of journalism, where I was taught to ask Who?, What?, Where?, Why? I learned that information is sacred. Tell the truth and let the people read it. I came to the city, and in three years I was this paper's top investigative reporter. "Faber, you have a nose for the news," the editor would tell me, resting his warm hand on my shoulder.

Times have changed. Now I return with my copy and the editor yawns, the pages drift from his outstretched hand, down through the heavy air of his office, to join his leftover tuna salad in the trash. Yesterday he burnt a hole in my story with his cigar, and stared at me through the hole, wondering what I was doing there.

I cannot compete. The honest trade of reporter has become impossible to follow due to the total absence of news, a shortage created by a change in definition. Events still happen, stories are still lived, but nothing that actually occurs is spectacular enough to wake readers out of their trances.

"PLANET BREAKING UP, EARTH HAS 24 HOURS TO GO, SAY SCIENTISTS."

That one wouldn't lower the volume of one HomeEnt Unit in the big city. People don't give a shit for whatever reality struggles up and breaks the surface. Call 'em as you see 'em, and no one listens.

My editor, brilliant bastard that he is, faced with this difficulty, and the accompanying drastic drop in circulation, solved the problem.

He began by printing outrageously salacious gossip, hired a team of lawyers to handle the libel suits. Computers monitored the circulation figures hourly. Failure. He searched desperately for the lowest common denominator. One day he stepped over the line, deliberately "livened up" an otherwise routine burglary story. He added a transvestite and voodoo. The sales needle jumped.

The editor had found the answer. He began by sticking to tried and true themes: death in suspicious sexual circumstances, political hanky-panky, submarine disaster. It wasn't enough. He invented poisonous chewing gum, a nation of hermaphrodites, radioactive crabs. He created an entire set of famous celebrities, and the paper covered their fabulous doings in detail. These alternate personalities were just as good as the real ones—better, as they couldn't sue, and could be killed off with impunity.

It was still necessary, however, to maintain the appearance of fact, and the paper hired a specialist in producing soporific copy full of statistics to provide a reassuring glimmer of dullness, a stable background for the amazing scoops of the day.

It was one copy boy's attempt to satirize this emerging genre that finally put us over the top. The editor took one look, and printed it on page one. He had the genius to perceive that the paper had become invulnerable to satire, as we had already absorbed that function, had, in fact, destroyed the concept. Now, there were no lengths to which we could not go. Sales zoomed.

The only remaining problem was staff. When the editor hired the first full-time inventors, they masqueraded as feature writers, but he gave them a separate section on the floor. In three weeks they were in the city room, and the reporting staff was making daisy chains. These people were hired to manufacture events on an hourly basis. We were encouraged to follow their example. The editor gave us a pep talk about broadening the paper's scope, about serving the public. He pointed out the subjective nature of truth. One week later, all reporters still unwilling to apply their talents to the new methods of "news-gathering" were fired, except one. I have been kept on, perhaps to be pointed out as a vestigial organ that the paper, with its new prosperity, can afford to maintain.

I am still sent out daily on choice assignments: assassinations of entire football teams, complex cases of political corruption with exotic sexual backdrops, remarkable gymnastic performances by crimelords in abandoned warehouses, imaginative desecrations of churches and amusement arcades. These events I am to cover, however, have never taken place.

When I get there the sleepy security guard stares at me. "You crazy, Mister. We ain't been robbed since '97." Suicide laughs from behind his rosewood desk. "When I pull the trigger, Faber, I'll call you. Wouldn't want you to miss the blood coming out all over my suit." And the old ticket taker smiles—"Are you kidding, son? The season's over." These non-events are the editor's idea of an invitation. I refuse. If it didn't happen, I won't write it. We are both aware that therefore, I am useless, and it is only a matter of time before I am shifted to latrine duty, or sent out to sell it on a street where everybody's getting it free.

The industry followed our lead. *The Bugle, Clarion, Enquirer, Examiner, Globe, Herald, Journal, Mirror, News, Post, Register, Star, Sun, Telegram, Times,* and *World* now consist of the names of nonexistent winners of nonexistent lotteries, details of the imaginary sex lives of imaginary popular entertainers, births of freak animals, tales of homemade violence, battle reports and casualty lists of wars not yet fought, and round sums in dollars of monies won, swindled, or assessed for property damage.

My editor invents the sums personally. "I have a knack for figures, Faber."

Truth is no longer stranger than fiction in this sweet world of ours, and the editor knows it.

I'd quit if I could afford it, but I won't be a goddamn charity case. Meanwhile, I have dreams where I find the money to buy a newspaper. I print the truth and let people live with it. My presses are rolling, the paper's on the street—no one reads it, pages blowing down back alleys....

Those suckers who work for the paper now—not one is writer enough to lick my shoe. They all got one hand on some secretary's tit and the other on their lunch, mouth working into the desk mike. Soon there won't be any real story, if no one's telling it....I haven't read a newspaper for three years.

The moment that really scares me is when I realize that one of these inventors, who seems momentarily interested in my bitching and preaching, is actually amused, as if I'm an entertaining lunatic at a party.

So here I sit in the golden age. From my desk at the rear of the City Room, I occasionally fire paper clips at my creative colleagues, as I watch the news being made.

Faber at home. That's me. Project 1019, Unit D, Level 27, Aisle A, Apartment 33.

My door is steel, a rectangle of shinier metal soldered in place where the Ident lock system used to be. All the doorlocks were removed by government order five years ago. No longer needed. At that time, there'd been no criminal acts recorded for six months. There have been none since. The prisons are empty, the police force disbanded. The name for this miracle is "chemically-assisted reconditioning" of criminals. Let me put it to you another way: one dose of Stelbesil B and any thoughts about someone else's HomEnt Unit or someone else's body or someone else's cufflinks—these thoughts just fade away. You don't want anything bad enough to do more than stretch out your limp hand for it. So here we are, safe and sound.

Evenings, a delicate blue hum rises out of the HomEnt Units, diffuses in a nimbus around the buildings. The Project is vibrating gently. The world feels faintly electric. Ten thousand minds with but a single thought. Fun time. Laughter from across the courtyard, a scream through the wall. My fellow residents are busy demonstrating to each other their various successful modes of adaptation to life in this twenty-first century.

When I was nine years old, we left our home in one of the few countrytowns remaining. The water went bad, and there were no filtration systems outside the cities. My father got a job caring for the electrics in a city subsection. We moved here, Project 1019, Unit D, Level 38, Aisle F, Apartment 79. Door numbers kept being painted over or changed by unit goons with nothing to do and the world to do it in. A joke.

My mother taped a bouquet of plastic flowers to our door so she could tell it from the others. Someone stole it. She put up another. When it disappeared as well my mother ran sobbing to my father. She told him that she hated it here, and she wanted to go home. He held her on his lap like a baby, folded his arms around her. Nothing to be done.

From then on I held my mother's hand, her arms full of groceries, me with the Ident, groping in the piss stink hallways for the slot. I'd make a secret sign on the door every morning, look for it at night. A spider. Brave boy.

But I couldn't breathe. Rattle and wheeze, breath barely squeezing through my throat as if from inside I was trying to kill myself. They gave me pills. I threw them away. I was going crazy.

One day when I was fourteen I stole some money from a cash register in a DrugStop. I came home after midnight, left the money in a pile on my father's bed, and went to the door. I was leaving. I was halfway down the corridor, and my mother was suddenly there behind me, a small figure far down the hallway in her old blue nightgown. She watched me get on the elevator. They never knew where I went or how I cried for them after.

It was years later, when I'd gotten my job on the paper that I came back. Times had changed. The Project was sparkling with new paint. A computer signal system with colored lights guided you to your apartment. No Ident slots. All the tenants were new. Nobody remembered my parents. "Sorry, Mister...all gone now."

I can see them on the hill, my father bent almost double, leading my mother by the hand, black silhouette against a yellow sky, concrete roofs below, piss in the hallway, dead faces in an acid rain....

I moved back in. I'm still here. I flip a switch and the aluminum venetian blinds swivel shut. The place is dark, little fuzz of summer twilight where the blinds don't quite meet the sill. O.K. I mix a bourbon and water, flip off all the HomEnt inputs, stick an old cassette into the machine— summer, ten years gone.

I know this one by heart. Magic lantern slides from the land of the dead, all in living color, and a kind wind blows down from the last countrytown, carries these laughing ghosts back to me: Arlie, and the little one. She's three years old, making faces at her funny Daddy and his camera, hands full of blackberries.

Who is gonna be there to put honey on your grave? That's the question, and in my case the answer is no one. I've been alone for a long time. I've almost got used to me this way. If I had anyone else to worry about, I'd probably spend my days selling it with the rest of them.

We have peace, plenty, security—but somehow we got it backwards, and the concentric canals of this audition for Gehenna are filling up with corpses. I'm talking about an avalanche of corpses. Just tilt the streets and here they come. . . . This story originates direct from a spell-binding necropolis.

But I'm still hoping the doctor will show up, whispering comfortingly in my ear: "All this is just a fantasy of yours, Mr. Faber. An illusion. Once you understand that, you can go home."

There's a notion about the human mind that says it resembles a city if, instead of being razed and rebuilt time and again over the centuries, only the rebuilding occurs. The old structures never come down—old and new exist simultaneously, layer on layer, a two hundred level sky-scraper and a peasant's hut on the same spot, woven into each other. Bent crone in rags, basket full of mugwort, shambles into a high speed passenger elevator, all glass and stainless steel. Past and present exist together, with the latest layer as the visible facade, behind which stand the dens of the neanderthals.

Juicy notion. This city and its citizens stand to disprove it. Everything but the latest mind layer is rubble. All gone now—old witch lady, helmeted police, flashy prostitutes, ragged saints. . . . All that's left are the fun-loving citizens of the twenty-first century. They got the secret: total self-sufficiency—lives which, needing nothing, can never be disappointed.

And the old man keeps yelling from a flophouse window: "Bad times? Keep hid." I'll never learn that one.

On my way to work, I spot a stock of today's edition: "HINDU TRANSVESTITE HANGS SELF WITH TURBAN IN HEALTH SPA."

Business as usual. Another day on duty. And then suddenly the Editor himself appears in our parody of a City Room. He's in his knickers and a fire engine red vest. Its buttons are gold, each one depicting a different scene from a famous opera. He strokes his white moustache.

"Ladies and gentlemen of the press. At 9:01 this morning the island prison, New Jerusalem, opened its figurative doors to the remainder of the world, in which, if I am not mistaken, this newsroom is included. This is the first such opening in twenty years, the first since Arnheim's death. The United Nations, of which the prison is a trust territory, is closing it down, clearing off the population, and integrating them into society. I want a reporter on the scene."

Everyone stares into their laps. A real one. Work, and
then the story trashed or run next to the weather on the back
page. Their minds return to Jayne Mansfield's resurrection.

I think it through. Is this another game of the editor's?
"Sorry, sir. The information you have received that New
Jerusalem is open to reporters is incorrect. You are a liar or
have been misled. Now you will go home."

The city room is silent. I volunteer. It's what the editor
has been waiting for. His hands fly out from behind his
back, and in one bound he's on top of my desk, papers
scattering like ducks about his feet. His shoes are red.

"Faber! You're the goof-off of the staff. You don't pro-
duce! You sit there waiting for something to happen. Faber!
You're a fool, and you have the gall to volunteer to cover the
story of the decade! This takes flair! Insight! Genius!"

The editor jumps down, puts his mouth next to my ear. I
feel the heat of his breath as he whispers. "Do you think that
New Jerusalem is lying there in the sun, already invented,
and all you have to do is report on it?"

I got the assignment. This is the story.

BASICS: The penal colony that became New Jerusalem was
created forty years ago on a United Nations Trust Mandate
island. Criminals of all nations convicted of major crimes
were dropped there by parachute. No contact with the world
outside. No guards. No rules. No return. Live or die.

After ten years of this penological experiment, drug-
assisted reconditioning of criminals cleared the legal barriers
that had been stalling its widespread use. The island project
was maintained by the U.N., but no further convicts were
sent.

Some years later, the island was opened, at first only to relatives of prisoners. During this time it was discovered that its inhabitants called the place New Jerusalem. It had developed some odd architecture and customs, which prompted a mild wave of tourism. Certain disturbances, however, developed among the inmates, and all visits were abruptly discontinued. For the past twenty years isolation has remained complete.

I contacted the United Nations in the paper's computer room—took me two hours to locate which subsection of which bureau administered the island. When the screen finally lit up in the right office, a black haired woman with a thin nose looked out at me. The nameplate on the desk read "Miss Stanislaus." I asked my questions and she nodded, feeding a very thin file into the scanner. The printout next to me began to rattle.

"Tell me something," I said to her, "about New Jerusalem. Anything."

Miss Stanislaus looked up from the file. "Mr. Faber, all our data on the island are in the documents I'm transmitting."

I leaned in pleadingly toward the transmission eye. She looked me over, eyed her wall clock. She might just get rid of me before her lunch hour. If she didn't, she could tell I'd be calling back. I might even show up at her door.

"We're shutting it down, that's all. We're sending a ship to clear them off and recondition them. It was an experiment to begin with, and a very generous one at that. It worked, I imagine. No one escaped."

"But what happened there?"

"What do you mean, what happened?"

"To the prisoners."

"Nothing, so far as I know. They managed to survive. There have even been quite a few children born there. Paying for their parents' crimes, I'm afraid. The inmates get along, Mr. Faber, in their curious way."

Miss Stanislaus paused. "Mr. Faber, if Stelbesil B had not been invented, the U.N. would have run out of islands long ago." She's being defensive, and as I hadn't attacked her, I'm wondering why. I try putting it another way.

"Are you telling me that for forty years these people have been out of touch with the world, and nothing special has happened to them?"

"Not quite nothing. Did you ever hear of a man called Arnheim?" I remember my editor dropping the name.

"You will, if you're traveling there. Now, if you'll excuse me, I'm going to lunch. You've got all we have on New Jerusalem. I can add that it's hot as hell there this time of year." The screen went black.

Last night in America, studying up, copy of the New Jerusalem file all over the bed. Nothing much. Topographical maps of the island, financial statements, long lists of prisoners and their offenses.

The only incident covered in any detail is the rise to power among the prisoners of the man called Arnheim. One memo circumspectly mentions a suspicion that Arnheim was smuggling "materials" onto the island, including "electronic equipment." The committee resolution giving permission for the first small tour groups some twenty years ago, mentions that the prisoners, isolated for two decades, had developed an "interesting way of life." Due to this Arnheim's leadership and ingenuity, they were able to offer visitors some conveniences, and the sight of some odd types of primitive architecture.

Soon after these tour groups received U.N. travel permission, an incident referred to as "the chaos" seems to have occurred, coinciding with this Arnheim's disappearance, or retirement, or death.

Then, a twenty year blank—no information. The final document is the recent order to remove all prisoners from the island; test them; recondition with Stelbesil B where anti-social instincts and/or behavior are present; reintegrate them into society.

In other words, penological experiment abandoned. Though maintenance of the island costs nothing, the prisoners being left entirely to the mercies of each other and geography, the United Nations feels its continued existence is a mark of barbarism in an otherwise enlightened age.

I close the file, mix another bourbon and water. My one firm conclusion, out of this mess of data, is that the U.N. had no idea what was, or is, going on in New Jerusalem, and never bothered to find out. They didn't care, as long as no one escaped. The story's beginning to look like a live one.

HomEnt on, and I sit back in the blue wash of vidscreen light to stew in another of my replays. Cassette five—my daughter holds a white kitten, talks at the shaky camera eye.

"Daddy! Stop it. How can I play with Fiji if you're always

taking pictures of us. Fiji's sensitive. She doesn't like having her picture taken, even though she's so beautiful. Right, Fiji?''

And then Arlie waltzes across the back of the screen in a white flannel nightgown, doing a dancehall strut for the camera, holding a bowl of rice cereal in front of her like the head of Johnny Baptist.... So you see the dead come again to kiss me goodbye, last night before New Jerusalem. Ghosts come and kiss me all over.

Time to pack. One suit on my back, the other one in the grip. Shirts, underwear, socks, notebook. It doesn't seem like much, but I can't find anything else to take, and then I remember the gun, reach up to the very back of the shelf in the closet, take it out from under some sheets. It's a dusty Colt Python, an old snub-nose 38 revolver. I expect it works. I bought it years ago when I had something to protect, and before the crime problem disappeared. New Jerusalem's probably the only place left where I might need it. I wipe it off with a rag, and it gets shiny quick. I don't like the look of the damn thing. I toss it and a box of shells into my bag.

I want to tell you that this tale is true. I am not about to start inventing now. And it's not a story where an interesting point of goddamn view is set up by the writer through the use of a clever first person narrator, and so you're never sure of what the hell you're getting through this highly selective head. I am being honest as I know how, and will tell you where I go, and what I see.

You might go yourself someday, and could use the landmarks. Wouldn't want you getting lost. Guide book.

Back up on screen my daughter is walking along the Maine coast somewhere near Port Clyde, throwing shells back into the sea. The sky is light blue.

I refuse to become an entertainer. This is not coming to you prerecorded, from the showroom of the Splendide Hotel. This is coming to you live from downtown, and I hope we make it.

IN FLIGHT

Once communication developed to the point where everything but sex with another person's image was possible, transportation became less necessary. Most people stayed home, and the result is that travel has become a chancy affair. The airport, a late twentieth century wonder of glass and steel, was originally a passenger terminal. Now it has been altered to accommodate a huge volume of containerized airfreight, and a dwindling number of people. Escalators have been rerouted, ramps blocked, stairways sealed off to become storage facilities.

The waiting areas are rec-rooms for loading crews. I'm in one, lost already, and the trip hasn't started. Two hefty women play ping-pong in orange coveralls. I ask for directions and the one with the iron-grey hair turns to look me over.

"New Jerusalem Airlines? They back in business?"

"I hope so. I got a ticket."

She serves. Ace. "Try going through that Men's Room, out the door on the other side, left to Gate 31. Thought I saw one of their antiques pull in there this morning. If you don't make it off the ground, come back. You can play winners."

Once you're at the gate, things get worse. No announcement, no attendant, no sign. You get the sensation that time schedules and destinations might be changing from hour to hour, the pilots hired for their whimsical sense of time and place.

Then I remember that New Jerusalem Airlines ran the tour flights back during the brief time the island was open to visitors. This is their first flight in twenty years.

A small crowd gathers; a door opens. We board in silence.

The aircraft are the same as they were years ago—sloppily modernized B-52 bombers, with an eagle's head mounted over the pilot's compartment. When the planes are taxiing, these giant heads clack their beaks and roll their eyes.

The plane's interior is filthy—seats with their stuffing peeping out of the seams, floor littered with twenty year old coffee cups and newspapers. I find a seat, pull out the complimentary magazine from the seatback pocket in front of me. It is a copy of *Loving Couples*—looks like a badly printed hardcore monthly, published on the island itself by an outfit that calls itself Koon Wah Lithographers. First news from New Jerusalem, and I'm embarrassed to be seen

reading it. I tuck it into my inside jacket pocket. Later,
perhaps in the lavatory of the plane, I can look it over, get an
idea of these people's thinking—one side of it, anyway. The
first story seems interesting—a night watchman in a cellar
somewhere near the docks, and his erotic fantasies.

A dumpy middle-aged woman in dark glasses appears at the
front of the plane, a yellow cardboard megaphone in her
hand. The words "Welcome to New Jerusalem" have been
scrawled around the megaphone in black crayon.

The stewardess, if that's what she is, is brief and to the
point. "Fasten your seatbelts, and for God's sake, don't
smoke."

I look out the grimy oval window: blue flares along the
tarmac race toward each other. We slant upwards. The
plane tilts jerkily, banks, heads west. I'm looking down at
the lights of the city below, and something in me bubbles up
strong into my head. I press my nose against the plastic
window, stick out my tongue. I'm laughing without knowing it, and then I grip the seat arms to stop myself. I try to
breathe steadily, and in a moment I can.

I am just very glad to be going away. Down there the
wheels are spinning—belly-up on the highway, a siren
screaming. The driver's dead but the wheels go round,
touching no road, going nowhere, one long moment before
they stop.

The truth is that a lot of people figure they no longer have
to pay the piper in order to dance. It seems as if the
sonofabitch plays on anyway. He likes his job, or he's
drunk. Maybe he don't play quite as well as if someone was

paying, but play he does. Maybe the bastard is prerecorded, they got him on a tape loop, and he can't get off.

I look over my notes on New Jerusalem, and then the memory of the editor's grin as he handed me my ticket won't get out of my head....the son of a bitch. If this is one more of his gags I'll kill him—slowly—when I get back.

The place is there, anyway. It exists. Maybe I'll get lucky and the story will be flashy, sexy, and violent enough to print. Hell, with my luck, I'll find a couple thousand raggedy bastards chewing coconuts, just lined up at the dock, dumbly waiting for that boat to take them back to the land of milk, honey, and happy times.

At altitude and cruising. Across the aisle is a fat man, black-rimmed glasses, rumpled gray suit. He rolls his head toward me.

"Heading for New Jerusalem?" he says, and I wonder who's he kidding. Does he think this junker makes stops? I play along.

"Yes, I am." He looks pleased. We're talking.

"Say, I know who you are, Mr. Faber, and I'm not going to beat around the bush. I like your writing. Got the ring of truth to it. Thought I might try to make your acquaintance once I saw you listed on the flight record. My name is Petersen. I'm with the *Mirror*. Features—and this looks like a big one."

I'm curious where he's read anything of mine for the past three years, but not that curious. "Mr. Petersen," I tell him, "this is a long flight and I have a lot of work to do." He doesn't take the hint.

"You and me, Faber, we're the only newsmen aboard. The rest of them are seeing their relatives. No visiting time for twenty years now. They'll find things have changed a bit in paradise."

"I imagine."

I try to pay attention to a fat little cloud out the window, but Petersen is yelling at me. He doesn't seem to care that people are staring. "You could do worse than talk to me, Mr. Faber."

I turn back to him, embarrassed, and his voice softens, becomes confidential. He leans over toward me.

"I was in public relations before I started to write for the papers. I represented, among others, the New Jerusalem Tourist Promotion Board. Heard of 'em? I used to be their man in America in the old days, when Arnheim managed to turn a prison into tourist heaven. I believe they owe me. I got it in my files. So here I am, killing two birds with one stone, so to speak. I'm doing my feature, and going personal to collect. Something to tell the kiddies, eh? I'm going back on the ship that's taking everyone off the island."

"I'll be there till the end myself. I'm doing a story on the place, too. A kind of travelogue."

"Good, good. Love to read it sometime. I'm a fan of yours, Faber. So's my wife." Petersen takes a deep breath, and then he smiles. I can tell he's coming to the good part. "Let's be open with each other. I know that these days reporting isn't a job for a man who's done the work you have—and it isn't exactly the gravy train either."

"Mr. Petersen, lately, it isn't even the little engine that could."

"Believe me, Mr. Faber, I know it. I try to get some hard

news in, and I end up on the *Mirror*'s back page, under the tide tables. But I gotta admit I've invented a few good ones in my time. You read the series on the Peanut Butter Murders?"

"I stopped reading the papers a while ago."

"And right you are, too," says Petersen, "but when this New Jerusalem thing came up I jumped like a puppy for a biscuit. I figure, maybe there's something going on out there. Besides, I got a little advance information...."

Petersen lets me think that one over. I look up at the flaking olive drab paint on the passenger compartment ceiling, thinking how I'd like to buy a paper, even a goddamn weekly—use it to let people know something about how they live and who they are and how I see it—and then I'm thinking how I'd like to take this hack from the *Mirror* and shove him out the cargo door.

Petersen's voice interrupts this pleasant vision.

"You ain't prejudiced, are you?"

"Against who?"

"The citizens of New Jerusalem. Some people don't like them. Convicts, they say, and the children of convicts. Bullshit, Faber, and I'll say it again if you like. More decent hard working people you'd never want to meet. And you never would. But everybody is entitled to think what he likes, and you'd be the first to agree I'm sure. Think what you like, that's my motto. I think what you like. It don't hurt me."

He's made me curious enough to try to figure where his information's coming from. "Nobody's heard anything from New Jerusalem for years, even in the newsroom."

"Right, Faber," answers Mr. Petersen, and his eyes

widen behind his thick lenses, "but I've been a student of
the situation. I understand them, and it's simple, when you
think about it. After Arnheim died, New Jerusalem went on
retreat, as we used to say at school. Without the old man to
tell them how, everything just fell apart, and they said bye
bye for awhile. That's all. Just like anything else. Open,
shut, open. Think about it."

I do, until Petersen leans across the aisle to put his hand
on my knee. He pats it. "Mr. Faber," he says, "an
acquaintance of mine in New Jerusalem could do with a
little favor at the moment. Maybe you could help him out,
make yourself a little something in the bargain. Might be a
story in it."

"Mr. Petersen, why don't *you* do this little favor?"

"Chances, Faber. Chances. I'm not a man who takes
them unless I have to. You, on the other hand...."
Petersen pauses, considering something. Then he speaks
again.

"Where are you staying?"

"The Cockpit Hotel."

"What a coincidence," says Mr. Petersen. "So am I. Say,
can I borrow your copy of *Loving Couples*? I guess they forgot
to put one by my seat." I reach into my inside jacket pocket,
hand Petersen the magazine, and before you know it he's
asleep, the copy of *Loving Couples* on his belly going up and
down with his breathing.

Suddenly the plane's interior lights flicker out, and I'm
thinking the electricals go first, and we're on our way down
and out. Then a grimy screen lowers jerkily from the
ceiling, clicks into place.

The film is in faded black and white, shot badly with a hand-held camera. Something fills the screen that looks like the ocean in a worn print of an antique episode of *Victory at Sea*. Blurry titles flash on over the murk. They're in big white square cut letters, look like bright holes in the screen: "THE LIFE OF ARNHEIM." The letters fade out, others fade in: "A NEW JERUSALEM TOURIST PROMOTION BOARD PRODUCTION, Runme Singh, Proprietor."

Voice of a narrator comes out of the airplane's loudspeakers, an older man's voice, the extremely articulate phrasing of a ham actor. One more voiceover job. . . .

"One of the first criminals dropped onto the soil of the island prison, later to be known as New Jerusalem, was Arnheim, a convicted embezzler. In school, Arnheim was the child none of his playmates liked."

Murky background of ocean cuts to overexposed shot of woodframe house, smalltown USA. Cut to interior. Child's room. A shell collection on a table.

"He read too much. He collected shells."

A spindly hand reaches into the frame, moves shells dully from one spot to another. Background music fades in, oddly out of sync. It sounds like a Balinese version of *Rock Around the Clock*.

"At nineteen Arnheim was a junior clerk in a small trucking firm. Someone died, and he was assistant traffic manager."

And then I'm looking at a Sunday morning funeral in a weedy cemetery, the women in black veils, and a pine coffin is lowered. The preacher's mouth is moving but we can't hear him. The camera zooms in on a young man

toward the rear of the mourners, thick glasses, the be-
ginnings of a beard. He turns his face away.

"This promotion convinced Arnheim there were plans for
him in heaven. He began to study."

The narrator's voice drones on. On screen, blurred shots
of educational institutions, public libraries. Then book-
shelves, and someone's back as he reads a very large book, its
open pages covered with Egyptian hieroglyphics. We do not
see his face. A wall clock reads three A.M.

"Arnheim took up Greek, Hebrew, and Chinese, spending no less than ten hours a day outside his work in pursuit
of knowledge. His will power grew enormous. At one point
in his early twenties...."

The film switches from black and white to grainy color. A
small group of naked darkskinned people is sitting around a
fire on a sandy beach, cooking a large silver fish. One of
them laughs, flashing pointed teeth. Their voices are
garbled, in a language I can't understand. Close-up of an
amulet around the neck of an older woman. It's a scarred
tooth, and it hangs between her dumpy, dried-up breasts.
She waves at the camera.

"Arnheim translated the sacred writings of the Sea Dyaks
of Borneo, from the original dialect into English, and
published the work himself. It's been said that this book
influenced Arnheim to create New Jerusalem...."

Film switches to a black and white stock shot of the
ocean. A small boat bobs in the distance.

"...with its prophecies of a great city in the sea, 'the
House of the Dead,' that would rise at some unnamed future
time."

The narrator's voice is swallowed by the sound of drums

off an old jungle movie track, and the image shifts to a cardboard model of a tower—half dome, half skyscraper, on a blue table. The geometry of the structure is somehow all wrong, angles twisted, but before I can get a fix on it, the image fades to a blur, and the lecture crackles back out of the speaker. By this time, I'm taking notes as fast as I can, scribbling away in the dark.

"Arnheim's life from age thirty was devoted to making great sums of money, deliberately and surely. At forty he was one of the world's wealthiest individuals, and was prepared to realize his dreams. At forty-one, he was convicted of embezzlement. He was among the first to be given the new penological treatment...a life sentence to the island prison."

Corny patriotic music swells. Long shot of an airplane against the morning sun. A parachute blossoms like a flower, filling the screen.

"Arnheim, like the rest, was dropped by parachute. Below him were the previously dropped prisoners, waiting to strip him of his shoes and wristwatch."

Here the screen fills with smirking criminal faces, sneering and grunting at the camera. They are on a beach, in rags. One of them winks into the camera and laughs. The figure of a tall man in a white short-sleeved shirt and Bermuda shorts scampers out of the frame. He is wearing sunglasses, and has a clipboard. The narrator's voice begins to rise and fall like a preacher's. Music crashes into a kind of gypsy epiphany, as again we cut to the parachute falling.

"On the way down, Arnheim made a discovery. He had been sent to this island by God. He had set up his pipeline before he was convicted. His money on the outside would

spell: "PERFECT. THIS IS THE MOST WRETCHED
PLACE I EVER BEHELD." Again, the ragged criminal
types move threateningly toward the camera....

"Two murderers, a prostitute, a forger, an anarchist, and
two rapists came toward him...."

The menu board reappears. "I'M ARNHEIM. DO WHAT
I SAY AND YOU'LL GET ALONG HERE." One of the
criminals pulls a kitchen knife from under his shirt, waves it
about in an attempt to look menacing.

Then a round hole appears in this man's forehead. A look
of thoroughly realistic surprise flashes across his features.
The hole pulses with blood. He slumps to the sand. The
other three actors back away from the camera rapidly,
holding their hands up shakily in the air. The narrator's
voice picks up the tale again.

"Arnheim shot him through the head with a pistol he had
smuggled in, strapped to the inside of his thigh. He gave the
rest clasp knives and jewelry."

The three actor-criminals are running now, backs to the
camera, heading for a stand of trees some yards up the
beach. The camera cuts away to shots of construction work,
blueprints, scaffolding....

"After a time, no more parachutes bloomed in the sky.
The colony was ignored, and isolation was maintained. This
suited Arnheim, as he had some rather ambitious work in
mind."

We see buildings. These are in every style of architecture
conceivable: minarets, pueblos, domes, glass and steel
modern...an unbelievable jumble. Some of them seem very

real. Others look like stage sets, or models of paper mâché. Some buildings are shown in camera pans across still photographs, others in actual film, the whole sequence reminiscent of an incredibly sloppy travelogue of a demented amusement park.

"Arnheim's scheme for his city, to be called New Jerusalem, was complete: architecture, aesthetics, social planning, politics, religion. By this time, every convict on the island was totally involved with this vision of a paradise they would build with their own hands. Arnheim smuggled in only what materials were absolutely necessary. He didn't want his people contaminated by the "outside," as he called it. Work was unceasing."

Suddenly the screen goes blank. Then a stone railing appears, and a man standing by it in a black overcoat, his back to us, looking out into immensity. Clouds drift by. Then a scratchy recording of Bach's *Chaconne* fills the soundtrack. The narrator's voice has been gimmicked with an enormous amount of echo.

"Soon after the day of completion, as the streets were thronging with tourists, Arnheim died on the terrace overlooking his dream city. He blinked at the sky, felt a burp in his chest. He sank to his knees...."

The figure on the screen does so, still facing away from the camera.

"...and the last thing he felt was the rough stone of the parapet under his palm."

Close-up of a large and hairy hand, two jewelled rings, one on the thumb and one on the forefinger, gripping the stone tensely, then falling limp, slipping out of the frame.

"Arnheim's vision of New Jerusalem, a paradise for you, will live forever."

Triumphal music plays as credits fill the screen: "A NEW JERUSALEM TOURIST PROMOTION BOARD PRODUCTION, Runme Singh, proprietor. Directed by Sir Rodney Blessington."

The film runs out, clatters through the projector. The screen flickers to white, then black and we're in darkness. Snoring from somewhere. I put away my notepad.

I figure that Arnheim must have had his troubles, trying to divorce himself and his people from the "outside" and its cheap concerns. I can see him bouncing up, in that moment after death, into the white light, seeing a vision of the heavenly city, a parallel to his own. "As above, so below" he whispers to himself, and then there's Father George standing at the gate, his parish priest in a childhood he had invented for a press that no longer existed....

The plane's interior lights flip back on. Arnheim should have lived to be interviewed by Faber. But it's never too late when a real reporter arrives on the scene. I have it all...hand on the parapet, burp in the heart, black clot of blood on the horizon, far away.

I doze off for a moment, until the cabin speaker wakes me.

"This is your pilot speaking. Listen up. We are over New Jerusalem, and will be landing in a few minutes. If you want to see it before you get there, look out the window."

I do, and there's a featureless green dot on the sea. We're

circling. The speakers crackle with a sharp burst of static, and then a lazy voice from ground control.

"New Jerusalem Airport to 505, McPeak here. Howse it goin'?" McPeak has a southern accent. We can hear the pilot's response.

"It's going. Request landing sequence."

Squawks and static in response. Then a crash of glass, and McPeak screaming: "Kamoro motherfuckers! Get the hell offa there!" Sirens wail, and then the speakers click dead in the passenger compartment. They come back on with the calm voice of our pilot.

"I'm afraid there's a small disturbance on the ground. Baboons on the runway. They're a bloody plague out here. We'll be down in a jiffy, soon as they turn the flamethrowers on them. That is on your left. On the right, those of you seated on the right can see New Jerusalem harbor."

I am on the left. No baboons. A line of men and women is weaving across the airport's single runway, looking up at us as if to catch anything we might drop. They are being pursued by a van with a loudspeaker on top, which seems intent on running them over. The marchers break and flee....

We circle. Calm bay, tiny ships move slowly, a few clouds. One sampan below seems to grow larger. A Chinese family on deck is skinning a water rat. The rat has big eyes. A bright silver toy airplane appears in the center of each dead pupil. We touch down.

FIRST IMPRESSIONS

> ....*and, upspringing confusedly from amid*
> *all, a mass of semi-gothic, semi-saracenic*
> *architecture, sustaining itself by miracle in*
> *mid-air; glittering in the red sunlight with a*
> *hundred oriels, minarets, and pinnacles; and*
> *seeming the phantom handiwork, conjointly, of*
> *the Sylphs, of the Fairies, of the Genii, and of*
> *the Gnomes.*
>
> —Edgar Allan Poe,
> *The Landscape Garden*

I step out of the plane, down onto the runway—blinding
sun, grass breaking through the concrete, battered navi-
gation tower. The other passengers all seem to know where
they're going, and in a moment they're gone. I'm standing
there, suitcase in my hand, and I figure to take it a step at a
time.

I pass through the empty terminal, rusted luggage ramps,
one boarded up ticket window. Someone laughs behind a
door. In a small lounge at the far end of the terminal the

pilot and the stewardess are sipping brightly colored drinks through silver straws. Private party, I guess. A sign in front of the lounge reads: CLOSED.

I walk outside, and a row of antique taxis, Hudson Hornets painted gold, stands in the sunshine. It is a moment before I notice that there are no drivers. I look around. They are not shooting craps in a nearby alley. They are not anywhere.

Dead midday silence. I get into the front seat of the first cab in line. The key dangles in the ignition. The engine kicks once and purrs. What the hell. I pull out.

No signs, but no problem. There's one dirt road, and it begins at the airport. It must go somewhere. I'm driving, and I'm wondering ten things at once, including how the prisoners smuggled cars in, and what else I was expecting that wasn't gonna be that way. I figure I better drop whatever expectations I'm carrying, and just take in what shows up. . . be a lot less likely to get surprised or in trouble.

The dirt turns to cracked blacktop. Vegetation at the side of the road becomes sparser—shacks, tilled fields. Must be coming into some sort of town.

Then I realize that the road I'm on has widened, and the first in a line of highway lights appears on either side. I'm driving down a goddamn boulevard. Then, frame houses, a store of some kind, little kid playing in the dirt. Edge of town. Then, all at once, I come into the city of New Jerusalem.

Everything is like a dream of it, brown at the edges charred by a fire in your attic years ago. Niteclubs, barbershops,

formal gardens, grocery stores, restaurants, washing in the
wind—pool halls, parks, gazebos, casinos, chain stores,
palazzos, laundromats, drive-ins, docks, skyscrapers, tin
shacks from Rio, Navaho hogans built of coca-cola signs,
town hall from New Hampshire, courthouse from Spain,
pagodas, prisons, Metro entrances, escalators, elevators,
revolving doors, squares, cloverleafs, intersections, temples,
garages, shoe repair, sidewalk cafe, pawn shop—any city,
anywhere.

There are buildings all around me now, street signs, a
man in a doorway. I make a left, climb a steep street lined
with shops that seem to be out of an Alpine village on one
side and a Moroccan bazaar on the other. "COCKPIT
HOTEL" in neon blinks at me from the dead end.

I park the cab, leave the keys in the ignition. I set my
suitcase down, look things over. The hotel is brick, three
stories high, dominated by the giant neon sign on its roof.
The place is surrounded by weathered metal railings, covered
with ornamental ironwork, badly rusted and worn. The
pattern looks like grape vines, or long lines of a kind of small
animal I can't identify.

A ragged boy suddenly is squatting at my feet, shining my
shoes with a scrap of paper. He looks about six years old. By
him on the ground is a tray like the cigarette girl wears in
forties movies. As he shines he sings a little song:

"Shoelace, Green Spot, hairpin, guide book, 'larm clock,
chiclet." He raises his eyelashes at me.

"You for a free shine, sir. Every other one cashes on the
bucket, Mister sir. You for free. See your face in your eye.
Look under lady dress up. See poo-poo hair."

He shines on, his little back bent to his work. A small tattoo of a spider is on the back of his left hand. He spits carefully on each shoe in turn, begins his chant again as he rubs over the shoes with his palm. . . .

"Shoelace, chiclet. . . ."

"I'll take a Green Spot." The boy looks up at me again.

"Good pick, sir. Green Spot is a local soft drink, made of limes and spices. Not bad." His dirty hand is in front of my face, holding a small bottle full of dark green liquid. It's like drinking some odd kind of incense, thick and sweet.

"Timetables, Mister Man. Look." The "timetables" is a badly mimeographed sheet that lists the time it takes to get to New Jerusalem from almost anywhere else, by four modes of transportation: "feet, horse, bicycle, fly." There is no order to the list, so that the time from Montevideo by horse is listed after the time from the New Hebrides by jet, and before the walktime from Omaha.

I hand the kid back his timetable and a quarter. He disappears. I glance down at his work—see the blinking neon—"COCKPIT HOTEL," bounce in the shine. In front of the iron gate an old man wearing a general's uniform is asleep on a three-legged stool. He snores. I pick the key to the gate off a hook behind him, try the lock. It's already open.

I enter the lobby—potted palms, a chandelier. A man with a hat sits behind a newspaper written in a language I do not know. Seated on the floor, on one corner of the worn carpet, an old man in a violet bathrobe is contemplating his shoe.

The carpet is deep red, with a design motif repeated over and over in gold. It's faded and hard to follow—looks like a man in a fez chasing a wolf, who in turn is chasing a ball in flames. The lobby feels as if everyone and everything in it is coated with a fine layer of gray dust, with one exception: in a corner, on a worn plush couch, two women are talking heatedly. One is a tall Swedish looking blonde in a nurse's uniform. The other is small, dark-haired, with a pale face out of a nineteenth century colourplate. She's wearing a white silk shirt, so old it's turning yellow, with a spray of flowers stitched onto the back, and some kind of Turkish looking pants, gathered at the ankle. Her feet are bare.

I can't take my eyes off her. I'm staring and I don't care. It's easier to play the fool when you're away from home. I lean against a pillar, overhearing them in snatches. I catch something about a trip to somewhere that has not yet taken place. The dark-haired one, who can't be more than twenty, demands to be reassured, and the blonde is reassuring her. The kind of conversation where you're sure both parties are lying. They come to some kind of agreement, and they're laughing as they leave together.

They step out the door, and the little one turns her head toward me for one moment and, without breaking her stride, looks straight into my eyes. They're gone.

Above this scene, near the lobby ceiling, hangs a black outrigger canoe. In it are spears, netting, and five or six remarkably lifelike statues of paddlers, with a chief in the stern, and a guide at the bow. Probably a relic of the primitive natives who occupied the island before its heyday. The statues bend forward, muscles tense, their paddles digging deep into the waves. The chief appears calm, but the attitudes and facial expressions of the paddlers reveal their absolute certainty: something's gaining on them, and a moment's respite from fierce paddling will insure a horrible death. I spread the leaves of a potted palm, peering through at the legend pencilled on the pillar: "FISHING CANOE, NEW JERUSALEM ARCHIPELAGO."

I find the reception desk. Behind it, on a bench covered in red plastic, an anemic young man in baggy pants, a thin gray coat buttoned up to his chin, is curled up with closed eyes. There's a toothpick in one corner of his mouth, and his naked toes are twitching. I shout at the body, "Where's the deskclerk?" He sits up in one quick move, wide awake.

"I am it, Señor."

"I need a room." He looks surprised for a moment, staring at me. "We have a hundred rooms. Which one do you wish?"

I play along. "Number one."

The deskclerk laughs. "You must be kidding, sir." He reaches back to a rack of keys behind him, takes one in his hand.

"Number seven. Ten dollars in advance. And I'm required to examine your travel permit for New Jerusalem, entry documents, U.N. visitor number, and High School Diploma."

I hand him a twenty. It disappears into his pocket and he hands me the key and a pen. I sign the register, and he studies my name as if he's sure it's a phony.

"In your case, Messieur, we'll forget the official papers. But I must know if you intend to masturbate in the room. That's three dollars extra...."

There's no answer to that one. I just look at him, trying to get across the message that I'll twist his scrawny neck if he fucks around anymore.

He looks up at the ceiling, letting me know the small talk is over—but I'm curious. I tell him the hotel is lucky to have come across sculpture like the canoe.

"You think so, Messieur?" The clerk rests his pointy elbows on his desk, cups his hands, and rests his chin on them. "Odd you should mention it. Sir Rodney, the film-maker in Penthouse B, also inquired about the canoe. He wanted to buy it. Said he had friends in England it would be certain to amuse. Probably going to set it in the front parlour and have tea. Wants to take it back with him on the ship. I told him it wasn't for sale."

"Is it?"

"How would I know, Señor. I'm the deskclerk." He glances contemplatively at the end of his toothpick. "Sir Rodney refused to let me hear his radio, so I told him what I told him. I can see you're not that type of man."

"His radio? I was told not even a crystal set or an electric hot plate was allowed in New Jerusalem."

"Smuggling. We're a resourceful people, sir. Or were."

"You don't say," I tell him. He spits on the floor at his feet.

"There are three radios on the island at present. Two are out of order. The third is Runme Singh's, and he's loaned it to Sir Rodney. He listens to it with his brandy and soda, as he studies his idiotic shooting schedules. I heard it once. Listened through his door from the hallway. The sound is blurry, can't even tell what continent the broadcast is coming from, and the language was one I didn't understand. Pointless. Sir Rodney, however, doesn't care."

The deskclerk hits a small brass gong. A bellboy arrives from nowhere, face like a walnut, wearing a saffron yellow turban and knickers. He hops about like a half-dissected frog, giggling and showing his gums.

"You got wife, Sahib? You got camera?"

I shake my head, and he grabs my suitcase. I follow him. He stops before a door like the others, putting down the suitcase and hopping suddenly again, blinking his eyes. He taps the notebook in my pocket, and a sly grin crosses his face.

"You want ink monkey?"

"What?"

"Ink monkey."

I don't know what the hell he's talking about, so the best bet seems to be "No thank you." He taps my notebook, shaking his head in disbelief.

"Write, yes?"

"Yes."

He shakes his head again, shuffles off down the corridor. The room comes up to expectations. There's a bed, dresser, rusted cold water sink. The proprietor of the Cockpit Hotel probably stopped caring about twenty years ago, when the tourist flow was cut off. Long time to wait for business. Service gets sloppy. They probably keep the place open out of habit—or hope.

I later discovered that belief in the ink monkey is common in New Jerusalem. The creature is described as about four inches long. Its eyes are like carnelians and its hair is black and sleek. It delights in eating any sort of ink, especially the thick Chinese kind, but will also suck on the tips of ballpoint pens. Whenever people write, it sits with folded hands and crossed legs, waiting for the writing to be finished. Then it drinks up the remainder of the ink; which done, it squats down quietly as before.

Exhausted, but can't sleep. Late drink in the hotel's excuse for a cocktail lounge might help to wipe me out. I head downstairs with the U.N. file under my arm—bedtime reading. I pass the desk, check the register. Petersen has signed in below me.

My bellboy is tending bar. I get a drink, turn to the one document in the file I'm still puzzling over. It's clearly a map of the island, but the geography is overlaid with a kind of grid. There's a key below, indicating certain markings as antennas, coherent signal detectors, a power plant, imaging computer, optical systems, connecting service tunnels. Could be a surveillance system, could be a fancy version of an electronic barbed wire fence, could be a plan for complex air routes over the island.

A tall man with a moustache is looking over my shoulder. He has a Green Spot in one hand, and a short oriental woman in the other. "Curious," he says, and the word hangs there on his lips. He places his hand in the small of the woman's back, against the red silk of her kimono, and shoves her off toward the bar.

"Miyoko, my dear, I'll rejoin you in a moment."

She's gone, and he is grinning at me under the moustache. There are wide spaces between his yellow teeth. He's very drunk.

"I'm Sir Rodney Blessington, the filmmaker, and what you seem to have there, Mr....."

"Faber."

"Mr. Faber, is an actual schematic of the Ring of Fire. Where did you get this?"

"From the U.N. offices."

"I see. You are just arrived...to see us off, so to speak?"

"Yeah. I'm a reporter. But all I've got is a picture I don't understand. What is this Ring of Fire?"

"A device, Mr. Faber. A little something to make certain that none of us are able to leave our little paradise. Buoys are set in the ocean at intervals around New Jerusalem, and they generate an electrical wall. It is dimly visible in mist or heavy rain, as the vapor picks up a shimmer. This wall is deadly at touch. It was designed to be triggered by men, no matter how well shielded or concealed. Birds and fish pass through freely. It extends upwards about one thousand yards from the sea, and above the center of the island it curves into a dome, so that even if the most ingenious prisoners manufactured a balloon device, they found the air as closed to them as the sea.

"In the early days of New Jerusalem, this route was attempted by a few enterprising convicts. The result was invariably the same: a new star in the heavens. A burning man hung in the sky."

The speech is an effort in his condition, and Sir Rodney leans back in his chair. The woman called Miyoko steps in behind him, massages his temples lightly with her fingers. His eyes are glazed over from alcohol and god knows what else. Sir Rodney is smiling to himself. . . .

"Arnheim was a clever bastard, Mr Faber. Tell that to your newspaper. Figured everything out but how not to die. Arnheim sold us the myth of the impenetrability of the Ring—needed us inside to build his little world, needed us to live in it. Yet *he* got anything from outside his insane schemes required. There was a way."

Sir Rodney jabs one long finger at my chart.

"Here! The Ring extends only fifty feet *below* the surface of the sea. The designers no doubt imagined no prisoner would be able, with the material available on the island, to build any kind of submersible vessel. They were right. Nothing from outside has come in since Arnheim's death.

"Arnheim simply had his agents on the outside buy a submarine, buy its crew and their silence, and then built a submarine pen camouflaged from the air.

"He could have escaped anytime. He had no wish to. The great Arnheim could import whatever *his* constructions demanded. He didn't want the rest of us contaminated by random artifacts from the outside. No decent whiskey, no telephones, no *film* . . . ."

Sir Rodney suddenly stops talking, as if someone had pulled a string inside.

"Reporter, you said?"

"Yes."

He stands, drapes one lanky arm over Miyoko's shoulder. She stands very still and upright, supporting him.

"Perhaps I've been indiscreet about some ancient history." Sir Rodney has moved behind Miyoko now, his head bobbing over hers. His chin touches the part in her black hair.

"We're checking out of here in the morning. Goodbye." says Sir Rodney, "and perhaps I'll meet you on board the ship." I can see he's hoping he won't.

Colt Python tucked under the pillow, notebook open on the nighttable. A sound like a train whistle far away before I close my eyes.

To sleep—dreams of New Jerusalem, formal garden in ruins at the end of a long pathway, clouds moving rapidly across the sky. Statue of Apollo, nose and penis broken off, white blotches of marble. Time stop. Scars. Light rain. Scars on the statue of Apollo, formal garden, New Jerusalem. A head is floating, under a copper sky. A giant figure of a rooster strides across the horizon...COCKADOODLEDOO! Plumes of smoke from cookfires, chimneys, I see it all from my window, city of New Jerusalem. A flight of headless angels across the morning sky—rosy flush of dawn.

I lie here and look up at the ceiling, light coming through the venetian blinds. Morning, and now to begin. A true story. This is the final tale, front page. I am gonna blast those hacks off the map. I am gonna blast their cute little sex and horror lies off the map, crumble that dark arcade of dreams. You got eyes. See the words. Faded. Here we go. Read'em and weep. This is the ink monkey's last sip. Reporting. New Jerusalem serenade.

IN THE HALLS OF POWER

Be not afeared; the isle is full of noises—
—Shakespeare, The Tempest

First cigarette, smoke curls into the sunlight. Smells of unfamiliar cooking.

Curious dream last night. I dreamt I woke up, and a head was floating at the end of my bed. I'm sleepy and unable to make it out clearly. I can see the moon, very bright, through the venetian blinds. Its blue light falls on one side of this head, leaving the rest in shadow. My right hand creeps out from under the covers toward the pillow and my revolver under it. The gun in the dream is a Colt Python like my own, but brand new, freshly oiled and very shiny. Blasting the head will be a pleasure, however noisy. The head just floats there. My finger hesitates on the trigger. The hotel might have questions, complaints.

My senses clear, I can see the head is made of tissue paper, crumpled into a ball. It has risen now, about six inches above the bed, and is advancing along my body, as if to come and kiss me. Suddenly it speaks, the mouth flapping open and closed like a marionette's. The voice is a woman's, sexy out of a cosmetics ad, with slight oriental accent.

"Hello, Faber. Sorry to meet you here, so far from your home in America. You should be on the farm, taking a walk with your girl, doing the chores, sitting down to supper. Or walking down Broadway, seeing a show, sipping a coke. This island where we live, is where you die."

The mouth snaps shut. The head moves again, until it bobs over my chest, begins to revolve, spinning into a blur. The gun is in my hand as I stare at it, and a song is racing through my head.

I woke up. My gun was in my hand. Could have shot my toes off. The song, I cannot remember. We all have these odd dreams at times, especially in strange beds, first night in a new town.

Breakfast of papaya and oily coffee with a dessicated vanilla bean floating in it. My stomach's jumping. The waiter is the bellboy-bartender from the night before. He puts down the tray, winks at me, holds up five fingers.

"Five days," he says. "We all go home." Information seems to get around here, and I'm wondering how.

"Who told you that?"

He looks at me slyly. "Runme say so on his talking. Is it better home, or New Jerusalem?" I can't tell if he's kidding or retarded. "I don't know," I tell him, "Depends on your tastes. . . ."

"They have electric things for everyone, true?"

"Yeah. All you want."

He takes that in, then begins to giggle as he backs away. I can't tell if he's happy or he thinks I'm funny.

I look down at my notes, a little history before the intrepid reporter sets out to find what he can find. . . .

The original inhabitants of this island were Malays, Javanese, Indians, survivors of the wrecks of China Sea pirates or their victims. They met on this shore through acts of God, and mated with pygmies. The resulting and original citizens of New Jerusalem were short, and their gums were yellow. They filed their teeth. Once Arnheim was organized, he slaughtered them, and puzzled over where to dump the corpses, as he did not wish to defile his sea or his land. He burned them, and on hot days the stink is still there at the place where the charred bones are buried, beneath what is now the government center.

Fine. Just where I'm headed—the halls of power. If I can find them. I walk down a sidestreet to Phoenix Road, go left on Arnheim Boulevard. White pavement, weeds sprouting up through the concrete, on past an apartment complex, down a ramp into a public square: kiosks, Parisian urinals, pushcarts. There are peddlers of odd pink fruits, racks of badges of trades and organizations unknown to me, vials of colored syrups, firewood in stacks.

Beyond the square I spot a row of imposing buildings, British colonial style. I look around for someone to ask my question to. The obvious candidate is an old man covered from head to foot with maps, clipped by wooden clothespins to his faded tweed overcoat. I point to the buildings.

"Is that the government center?"

He hands me a map as an answer, holds out one brown hand. I try dropping in a quarter. The moment the silver hits his palm, he's talking in a tense whisper, pressing himself against me, though there's no one within yards of us. He stinks of fish.

"Your map is published by the Tourist Promotion Board, Runme Singh, proprietor. Every street is carefully named and marked, but the traveler will soon discover that the map is a blueprint for a future order, rather than a record of current reality.

"There are few street signs. Many of the roads do not exist. The map is dotted with rotaries, built with statues in their centers commemorating great moments in the history of New Jerusalem. After Arnheim died, the materials to complete this civic improvement suddenly disappeared, so that these circles are not connected with any neighboring roads. But one has only to ignore them, as the possibility of going forever around one looking for a way off is eliminated by there being no way on."

One skinny finger touches a spot on my map where there is a small line drawing of a building, row of columns down the front. He looks over his shoulder, whispers again.

"Government center. Just across the...." Suddenly a speaker atop a thin pole in the center of the square crackles with static. The mapman takes a step back from me, holds himself stiffly erect. His voice is suddenly loud and clear. "The map is excellent. Excellent. It's travelers who make trouble for themselves."

From the speaker on the pole comes an older man's voice, oily, strong.

"This is Runme Singh, proprietor, New Jerusalem Tourist Promotion Board. I invite you all to take a holiday to the wonders of New Jerusalem. Pay no attention to Kamoro cult propaganda. These are irresponsibles, radical students led by maniacs, who try to accuse this Tourist Promotion Board of merchandising our culture, of creating false traditions, of building exotic sets, unauthorized by Arnheim's plan, in which no one lives.

"This is lies. They are envious of our success in making New Jerusalem more attractive to distinguished visitors by modern methods. Crackheads! You can prove it to yourself. Chewing gum? Never. Cigarette butt? We clean up all kinds: Players, Lucky Strike, Gaulois, Del Prado, Pyramid Special.

"Safe and Sound. No gangsters shoot you in New Jerusalem. See the sights. You'll find them. Do not patronize unlicensed guides. Keep away from baboons and Kamoro cult practitioners. I am Runme Singh. Have a good life in New Jerusalem."

The speaker goes dead, and I look around. Everybody's going about their business. They've heard that routine before. Maybe it's tape. In any case, time for me to see if I can catch him live. The mapman bows, points me politely toward the government center.

The Runme Singh story, good as I can get it second-hand, goes like this. After Arnheim died, a small group of older prisoners, headed by Runme, who'd been the old man's shoeshine boy, emerged as leaders of the government. Their

only purpose was to expand the tourist industry. They
figured once the U.N. saw how good they were going,
they'd put the whole island in the cancel file, and they'd all
be back in the big city, next to a warm HomEnt Unit.

The Tourist Promotion Board, consisting of Runme
Singh and his cronies, became the only functioning organ of
government in New Jerusalem. It was fated to fail through
their corruption, incompetence, and greed. Once a few tales
of con games or street violence filtered back home, all
tourism was shut down by the U.N. The other social and
governmental structures of New Jerusalem began to collapse
on their own. Arnheim's paradise faded day by day, until
what remained was a twisted shadow play of itself, twilight
in the empty cinema, slow creak of the projector swiveling
toward the tattered screen; rusty sprockets grip the film one
last time.

New Jerusalem officials became the world's most bribeable.
In fact, they are positively eager to take a bribe, no matter
how small. The story is that often the offer of the bribe is
enough for policy to be changed in your favor, and the actual
bribe is unnecessary.

What they value is the feeling that they are able to have in
Tourist Promotion Board meetings that they have put one
over on the other members. Since all have this feeling, the
meetings are models of sly courtesy and decorum.

It is impossible for any government decision to be made
except out of a bog of self-interest, indebtedness, scheming,
blackmail, and lust. At the top of this slop heap sits Runme
Singh.

I walk up the marble steps of the government center. The doors are open. I walk through deserted hallways under sputtering fluorescents. A stray cat. I spot a travel poster, faded with age. In it a girl in a bikini is pointing at a large group of brightly painted statues engaged in a variety of daily activities: a merchant with his customer, a couple making love, a judge and a prisoner, two men arguing. Yet the figures all have their attention elsewhere, distracted, almost frightened. One or two look up at the sky. In small letters at the bottom of the poster: "SOUTH—DURING THE MONSOON." Across the top in giant letters: "WONDERS OF NEW JERUSALEM-3."

I walk on. Empty offices, file cabinets open, papers scattered across the floors. At the far end of the corridor, a man mops. He works methodically, sheen of wet floor behind him. He wears gray overalls and some kind of fuzzy cap; he bends over his mop as if he was painting the Mona Lisa in hot water on the tile. Slow.

"Excuse me," I tell him, but it isn't enough. I try it louder.

"Excuse me. I can't seem to find anyone. Is this a national holiday or something?" This works. He talks back.

"You see me mopping?"

"I'm a reporter. I'm looking for Mr. Runme Singh."

"No more. Buildings here are empty forever. I clean them. This is my last day, and I ain't quick, but I know this much. You wanna talk to me—you mop, I talk."

He takes the mop handle, slaps it into my palm, then closes my fingers around it firmly with both his hands. He sits down crosslegged on the floor alongside me. What the hell. I start mopping, and it's nice work. The mop slides

smoothly over the tile, clean smell from the bucket, wide arc
of wet behind. I'm mopping, and I'm listening.

"Few days, and we give this building to the spiders, so I'm
makng it clean for them. Spiders and snakes. Old Motorola,
he's gonna take up residence right in the boss's office, bring
his jewels and his golden stick. Government all gone.
Runme told me so. 'No more mop, Sammy,' he said, but
I'm mopping up for the spiders. You never know when you
need a friend. You need a friend?"

By this time I had mopped the whole end of the corridor,
and the janitor had slid along with me, using a queer
swimming motion along the floor. His voice grows louder,
throat muscles tense.

"Old Motorola, Betamax with his seven crowns, and
Magnavox his queen gonna sport in these halls. Red dust
gonna rise about their feet when they dance! They sent a
ship! Ship's coming, bringing Christmas every day—mix-
master—Chevrolet—toaster. Pssst!"

I stop the mop, look down at him. "Kamoro," he says.
With this word, the janitor points to his chest. He glides a
little further along the floor.

"You know Big Tiny? Tiny tells us lies from true." He
suddenly stands, and walks away rapidly down the long
hallway. He calls back over his shoulder, "Runme's home,
number one, Phoenix Road. No where else to go. Maybe
you get promoted. I'm gone. Mop or leave it to the spiders."

Runme's house—Spanish casa, with ante-bellum pillars out
front. Fat Mexican with a garden hose. A Filipino houseboy
is doing situps in front of the garage. I ring the bell.
Nothing. I ring again. I wait. The peephole clicks open.

Then the sound of locks sliding back, a steel bar being withdrawn.

The girl I saw in the hotel lobby opens the door. Her dark hair is a tangled mess of curls. She has a tiny puffy mouth in a pale angular face, skin pulled tight over the bones. Around twenty. A cross between a high fashion model and a Burmese monk. She's wearing a black cashmere sweater, tied up below her small breasts. On her belly I can see part of a tattoo of what looks like a panther. His open jaws must be biting on her right nipple but I can't see up there under the black cashmere, and she says, "Who are you?"

I say "I'm Faber, a reporter from America." She turns her head to look past me down the street, leaving her body facing me. The bones of her hips press against the silk of her blousy Turkish pants, gathered at the ankle.

"You alone?" she says.

"Yeah." Her feet are bare, toenails bright.

"Where's America?" she says.

I point east, try to smile at her. She's making me nervous.

"Runme Singh home?" Her answer is to spit on the ground between my feet. I jump and she laughs.

"I'm Margo. Follow me." Her voice is sweet and strange, each word comes out very distinct from the others. She has an accent, but I can't place it.

She locks the door behind us, sliding a steel bar in place. The house has been stripped bare. Rugs are rolled up along the walls. Piles of giant cartons are sealed, ready for shipping. Uniformed guards, machine guns slung over their shoulders, are shuttling from room to room with crates and boxes. They are dressed in striped pants with round tin helmets.

They manage to be tough looking bastards anyway. There are also guards stationed at the windows, machine guns propped on the sills, eyeing the street.

The floors are littered with straw, and objects not yet packed—a rusty gum-vending machine, a hair dryer, its plastic cracked and brown, cord clipped off short—and a row of five Mr. Coffee machines, still in their cartons. These are the only things I recognize. The rest seem to be broken chunks of wire and metal, whose function and/or beauty eludes me. There are also a few rough carvings in stone, one resembling a shark or dolphin. In any case, it looks like Runme Singh is planning to take it with him, what there is of it.

Margo's bare feet trace a path through the chaos toward one area of a central room that's clear of debris. She stops, cups her hands around her mouth, and yells at the top of her lungs.

"Daddy! There's a man to see you!"

Then she just stands there. I figure I'll make conversation. "Didn't I see you at the Cockpit Hotel the other night, talking with a nurse?"

"No" is the answer, and she turns her back to me. I feel a hand on my neck. A guard is behind me, and he slams a chair under my ass and me down into it. He lets his machine gun strap slip off his shoulder so he's holding it waist high, the muzzle about two inches from my breastbone. He looks nervous. Margo turns around and smiles.

"Wait here," she says. "I'll get him." Then the bitch giggles. She takes a step toward me and looks very serious, like a child about to recite in class.

"Daddy told me someone like you was bound to show up before we left. He's been dying to talk to the press."

I can't stop watching her till she's out of sight down a long corridor. Once she's gone I try exchanging pleasantries with the kapitan. I gesture to the pile of packing crates. "Moving?" I ask him, hoping he'll get the joke. No luck.

Click of bootheels, a door swings open. Two bodyguards, looking like extras in a foreign legion movie, charge into the room. One of them goes through my pockets, making me glad I was dumb enough to leave my revolver in my suitcase at the hotel. He looks in the cuff of my pants. He pats my legs and crotch. The other guard is busy shining his pistol barrel with his shirttail. He stops to admire his work.

Suddenly I notice a short dark man standing in the room, wiping the sweat from his brow with a purple handkerchief. He is in a shortsleeved shirt, wears a tie with a palm tree painted on it. He also wears wraparound sunglasses and an assortment of medals on his shirtfront. Runme Singh, I presume. Margo stands behind him, pointing at him, for my benefit, with one red lacquered fingernail. Runme turns to her, and in a whisper I can overhear. . . .

"The reporter?"

"Faber," she says, "from America."

Runme extends his right hand and marches toward me. Before I know it he is pumping my hand in his. His hand is sweaty. He opens his mouth to talk, then notices my notebook sticking out of my jacket pocket. He takes it out carefully, puts it in my hand. I manage to find the pen myself. He gestures to the guards. They step back from me, station themselves along the walls. Runme Singh is genial, to say the least. I take notes.

"I can't tell you, Mr. Faber, how relieved I am not to be governing this miserable island any longer. The difficulties I and my council faced day after day would amaze your readers. Not only did we deal with an ignorant and diseased populace, but we faced the added restriction of being, in fact, a penal colony. We were free, of course, but only within our limits.

"The people's craving for trade, for forbidden appliances, was enormous. They wanted tourists, as in the old days under Arnheim, but that too was not permitted by the outside. We did our best, but it was never enough."

Sudden noise from the street. Shouting, and then the crack of breaking glass. The guards stiffen, back in toward the center of the room, their hands tightening on their guns.

Runme is terrified. He drops onto his belly and crawls toward the window. A chant begins, low and far away at first, then swelling in volume. "Sannyo! Sann-yo! Magnavox! Magnavox!" is all I can make out as the chanting grows wilder, more confused. Runme's hands reach up and grab the window frame. He hauls himself up so that he can peep over the ledge. His whole body is shaking. He turns around toward me, beckoning hysterically.

I hit the floor, crawl to the window alongside him. He grabs hold of my arm, points to the street outside. I take a look.

A long line of men and women dance in the sun, weaving their way around Rumme's house, chanting "Sann-yo!

Motorola!" and god knows what else. Many of them are in old straw hats, sunglasses, shorts. Some have travel stickers and airline baggage tags hung all over them. One woman dances closer, and I can clearly see the letters LAX on a ragged pink scrap of paper tied in her hair. A man in a Hawaiian shirt, holding a battered suitcase, shakes his fist.

All the races and nationalities of the island population are out there. There are children. Around everyone's neck is a black box, hanging from a string or ribbon. "Kamoros!" Runme whispers in my ear. "Those black boxes are clumsy mockups of cameras. They all wear them. The Kamoro cult!"

"The tall one in front," whispers Rumme, "is Big Tiny, their leader. An intelligent man. He knows that the ship is coming in a few days. He understands very well that the U.N. will eliminate this island from the penal rosters, close it down. We will at last join the human race."

Runme Singh slides away from the window, presses himself against the wall. The chanting grows louder. A rock crashes through the glass and rolls to a stop. Runme is frightened, and furious.

"They actually believe that this is lies, that my government's final announcement was lies. Tiny tells them so. They believe the ship is coming, yes, but to bring at last all the appliances they have performed their magic to obtain. It is the apocalypse of their simple cult."

Runme is breathing heavily now, his eyes glazed, as if the words he speaks charge him, fill him.

"They believe the ship is filled with rotisseries, coffee makers, plate warmers, dishwashers, dryers, hairblowers, electric carving knives, pot scrubbers, toasters, telephones,

radios, television sets, entire cinemas, simultaneous translation booths, HomEnt Units, biofeedback units, lie detectors, stereo equipment, and motorcars."

Another rock smashes through the glass, lands at our feet.
Runme screams to his guards.

"Disperse the bastards!"

Bursts of machine gun fire, screams, cries of "Betamax!,"
"Death to Runme Singh!," "Magnavox!"...then quiet.
Runme relaxes, but only slightly. He's close to me and he's
almost shouting. His breath smells like Listerine.

"Big Tiny prophecies to them that when the ship arrives,
five thousand tourists will emerge from the red hot depths of
volcanic Mount Arnheim, and march into New Jerusalem,
spending money. They claim that I have enraged the
tourists, so that they hide from us under the earth. These
cult adherents have never cooperated with my government
for fear of angering these mythical tourists, who they believe
hate me. They claim that I am hoarding appliances and the
secret of how to work them. Madness. Do you see any
devices here?"

I figure all the stuff in the boxes isn't there. Runme Singh
leans over my notepad, sees my doodling: three fish and a
froggy. I reassure him by pointing to my head.

"I got it all up here, Mr. Singh." For the moment this
seems to satisfy him. He warms to his subject. In fact, he's
hot.

"At times the Kamoro cult has been so certain that the
tourists and appliances will come that they throw all their
food into the sea, and then the tourists do not arrive, their
gifts do not arrive, and the government has to feed them.

"Do you realize, Mr. Faber, that there is one admittedly

deviant section of this cult who believe that the tourists are already here, that they must only learn to understand this, to recognize it. Yet another splinter group believes that they themselves are the tourists. Perhaps you feel that these ideas would find no welcome in a healthy mind. Here, Mr. Faber, I agree with you. These people are insane. Are you listening?"

"I certainly am, Mr. Singh. I'm getting every word."

"Their twisted recollections of the outside, the pictures of toasters and headphones in faded magazines, the memories of tourists in Arnheim's time—these things have boiled together in their heads. Their rituals and prayers would be fertile ground for a scholar in lunacy, Mr. Faber—lunacy."

Runme Singh is pacing the room, bootheels clicking on the tiles. His face is sweating, and he wipes it with his purple handkerchief. He forces a chuckle, and it's clear he doesn't think what he's about to tell me is funny at all.

"Mr. Faber, they even believe there is a child who will lead them to their paradise—Big Tiny's son. He's been raised for this purpose from birth. They call him the Kephiboy. Big Tiny tells them that the child commands a number of spirits who sail the seas about New Jerusalem in boats with black sails, each armed with a flowering stick that has the power to cause any dolphin who smells it to follow its possessor. Under this spell, the unhappy beast swims along to shore, where it is netted, and carried to a clearing far from any human habitation. Here the spirits seize the living fish and bore a hole through the top of its skull. It is then suspended, head downwards over a caldron of boiling oils. The drippings from the dolphin's brain fall into the hot oils and supposedly form a most valuable medicine, known as Kephi, or the Extract. Thus, the Kephi-boy. Quite a fairy-tale, yes?"

He doesn't wait for an answer.

"This is bad enough. But the cult also believes that only this medicine can cure the members of my council of the effects of our supposed dissipations. In fact, they believe that I myself cannot live a day without this extract. Idiots. You understand, of course, that all this is a fabrication imposed on them by their leader, who finds it necessary to discredit myself and my colleagues."

Margo waltzes back in, steps between us, a bottle of green liquid in each hand. Runme grabs one greedily, puts it to his lips. Margo hands me the remaining bottle.

"Green Spot," she says. "A local soft drink made of limes and certain spices."

I take a sip. "Not bad," I tell her. Runme is winding down. He's thoughtful. He gestures at the guards. They snap to attention, leave the room. It's the three of us now.

Margo is waiting patiently. She probably came back for the good part. Maybe they'll shoot me. Fantasy of someone with a gun in my face screaming, "Faber, you know too much!" and me trying to explain that I've understood absolutely nothing, hoping my stupidity will save my life. Runme interrupts this pleasant vision. He's back to his genial self.

"Perhaps you can do me a small service, Mr. Faber. It's difficult for me to venture out into the street these days. The Kamoro cult is quite anxious to murder me. There's a package being held for me by a friend of mine in his office...Dr. Leroy. If you'd be kind enough to pick it up for me, I'd appreciate it. Margo, my daughter, will direct you to make certain you don't get lost. The package is a memento of my long stay here. I should hate to leave without it."

I'm listening, and thinking, and I remember Petersen's friends who could "use a little favor." I'm looking at Margo and I'm thinking she doesn't look like anyone's daughter, especially Runme's. The whole deal sounds phony...but she's part of it, and besides, there might be a good story angle. I wait to see if there's more to the pitch. There is. Runme twists his fingers together, untwists them.

"In a matter of days we leave here, Mr. Faber. Certain things need to be arranged during that time. The help of a man like yourself would be invaluable. You'd get your story from the inside...and believe me, it will be worth your while. I don't know what you like to buy, Mr. Faber, but I promise you that when the ship arrives in the other world, if they still have things to buy there, I'll personally make sure you have your choice...."

Money. Visions of chorus girls, a new place to live, firing the editor and buying the damn newspaper—all flicker through my head at once. I take another look at the sweating Runme Singh. He's worried—and then he sees I'll do it, just before I say it. He grabs my hand, holds on to it tight, then abruptly lets it go. I ask him, "Do you know a man named Petersen?" Runme gives me a blank look that seems genuine.

"Never heard of him."

Margo smiles. "I could show you the leprosarium while we're at it. Doctor Leroy is really quite a genius in his line...." Runme smiles over his Green Spot. We're a cozy threesome. He puts a hand on my shoulder.

"Quite a girl, Margo. Born here, you know. Very eager. You're the first man from the outside she's ever met. Let's say you're the first man she's been acquainted with who has not yet been convicted of a major crime.

"Bring back my package, Mr. Faber, and I'll tell you some secrets." He pauses to chuckle, way back in his throat. "Full face, and profile."

MEDICINE

According to report, before you have reached the island, it looks like a cloud. The living creatures, both birds and beasts, are perfectly white, and the palaces and gate towers are made of silver. Many immortals live there, and the drug which will prevent death is found there.

—Chhien Han Shu,
trans. Chavannes

The city of New Jerusalem smiles, like an orangutan sucking on a radish. Far off second story window, old victrola playing the Beatitudes. Margo and I walk rapidly down toward the dock area of the city, heading for Dr. Leroy's medical compound. We come to the bank of a narrow river, walk up onto a stone footbridge. A sign at the entrance reads: "The Bridge of Monkeys." Below the sign is a metal box, with what looks like a speaker grill on one side of it. A tin statue of a monkey, his face in a hideous grimace, is sitting on top of the box.

"His paw," says Margo. I give her a blank look. She laughs, reaches out, pulls the monkey's paw sharply downwards. A low mechanical voice from the box begins to lecture me.

"The New Jerusalem River runs through the city, and is crossed by seven bridges. The Bridge of Monkeys, the Bridge of Teeth, the Bridge of Progress, the Bridge of Sand, the Bridge of Snakes, the Bridge of Love, and the Devil's Bridge.

"Beyond the river's mouth, in New Jerusalem harbor, is a mechanical dragon of the oriental kind. He raises his head from the water at dawn, steam gushing from his nostrils. He blinks his eyelids slowly and lowers back into the bay. The mechanism has worked faultlessly for twenty years, sealed at the bottom of the harbor."

"Only a few of these boxes left," says Margo. She takes my hand, draws me on across the bridge. "Left over from Arnheim's time. He put them up for the tourists."

"Were there a lot of them? Tourists?"

"Don't know. Before I was born. I never saw one. Except you." She laughs. We pass between rows of stone monkeys on the bridge railings. All are in different positions, but have the same attitude—trying to reach up and catch something in the air above their heads.

"What are they doing?" I ask her.

Margo laughs again. "Trying to grab the moon."

We walk on, down back alleys, past empty warehouses, shuttered luncheonettes. We reach a row of long low buildings, like quonset huts open on the ends. Dark tunnels sitting in the sun. We walk by the first of them, and the stink is overpowering. A man in a bloody apron is standing in the entranceway, and the skinned carcass of a small crocodile is lying on a cement slab alongside him. Blood drips into a trough around the slab, feeding into a pipe leading to an open gutter that runs the length of the shed. The man wears his thin skinning knife on a leather strap at his belt. He looks up, his dead blue eyes catching the light. He nods at Margo. Suddenly she stops walking, and I brush up against her. I can smell an odd perfume in her hair, like almonds. She talks softly. "We're invited in...just for a moment."

We step into the darkness of the shed, and my eyes adjust. The man in the apron is about six-two, with blond curly hair, and a vacant, handsome face. Behind him down the length of the shed are other cement slabs, other men in bloody aprons, skinning out other crocodile carcasses.

Margo makes the introductions. "Mr. Faber, this is Harry—Harry the Horse. He's the foreman. Faber's a reporter from America, here to see us off."

Harry takes a step toward us, brings his left hand up in front of his face, fingers spread wide. In his right hand is his skinning knife. Suddenly the knife skids down between Harry's middle and forefinger, nicks open a vein. The blood dribbles down his palm, and he holds it up toward me. I'm staring like a fool, and Margo digs her elbow into my ribs. I notice her bare toes are caked with dirt and blood. She grabs my hand, nods at Harry, as if acknowledging something for the both of us.

She drags me out of there, and I'm asking questions.

Margo tells me that Harry the Horse, like everyone else who's got the message straight that life in New Jerusalem is about finished, is anxious not to go back outside empty-handed. He's saving up for the return to the world, so he can buy a bar and grill. He was displaying his talent for us, in case we wanted to hire him.

We're walking, and she tells me Harry's story, and now I'm telling it to you.

Harry's is the career of a man who took advantage of his aptitudes. He is the valuable commodity known in phony hypnotist circles as a horse, a man who cannot feel pain. He can be burned with the candle flame, pricked with the pin, the needle can go through his cheek, or if it's a small town and they'll take it he can be cut lightly with the straight razor, being careful he don't bleed too much. Harry keeps his eyes closed and feels nothing. A good horse is hard to find, and usually takes half.

Harry is from the USA, and worked for years with a Doctor Walford Bodine, mostly American Legion Halls in the Southwest, and up into California. He had a legit booking one night in the Los Angeles Coliseum as opening act for a lousy rock band, the triumph of Bodine's career. The Doc was up there on the stage and asked for that vital volunteer from the audience. Harry was drunk in a hotel room in Echo Park.

Bodine tried it anyway, and when the sucker he called up on stage went under, he felt he might get through. When the candle flame got two inches from the volunteer's palm he screamed bloody murder, and they laughed the great Walford Bodine off the stage.

After the show, Bodine came looking for Harry the Horse with a hypodermic full of chloral hydrate. Harry had to break his neck with his bare hands. Three weeks later he was descending into New Jerusalem, lights of Cowboy Dreamland below. He was the last to be consigned there....

Harry's talent is serenity with a vengeance. He's been left in nirvana by his nervous system, without a dime for carfare. When Harry speaks the topic is always an immediate need that, due to circumstances, he cannot satisfy for himself. Occasionally, Margo tells me, to satisfy these needs in New Jerusalem, Harry does favors. Anything, if the price is right.

According to Margo, rumor says he's good. He waits, like a stone frog on a mudflat, motionless until the moment to strike, then his tongue flashes red in the light, and he's gone. He doesn't think about it at all.

Margo points into the distance. "Dr. Leroy's compound is on the outskirts, down by the water. Not much further, Faber, and you're seeing the sights, what there is of them."

We pass by a long alleyway. I stop to peer down it, and see that the fronts of the houses are covered with flowers. The alley reeks of their heavy perfumes: jasmine, honeysuckle, orange flowers, scented orchids. Margo doesn't want to stop. The place makes her nervous, so she's tugging on my arm, pulling me away from the alley, when a man slides out from behind a red door covered with gardenias. He wears a flat black hat, and a black suit of some shiny material. He has a tiny moustache.

The man holds up a paper clip chain. On the end of it is a tiny silver bear that glitters in the sunlight. He holds up another chain, made of pieces of bamboo strung together.

On the end of it is a flap of skin, with white and black hair growing out of it.

"For a friend of Margo's, special price."

I found out later that the profession of amulet-maker is a common one on the island. The amulets are always intended for protection against enemies, sickness, and sudden death. They're big sellers in New Jerusalem, where the need of everyone for powerful defenses, the traveler in particular, is assumed.

As I'm saying no to the amulets, a dog barks from behind the door. Then he pushes it open with his nose, a mangy spotted little animal. The amulet-seller quickly turns, tries to shut the door on the dog, as if his presence would be an embarrassment or bad for business. The dog growls, slides out quick, and goes for his leg. The man swings his shiny shoe, kicking the dog with all his strength. The poor little bastard goes flying.

The dog lies belly up in the dust, its tongue hanging out of the side of its mouth. The man brings his heel down on the dog's skinny ribcage. The dog screams, I swear. I grab the bastard by the shoulder, pulling him away from the animal, and throw him down into the street.

Then there are faces at every window, and Margo has me by the arm. I can feel her breath in my ear. "Asshole! What are you doing?"

"I don't like seeing animals mistreated."

"Mistreated?" Margo repeats the word as if it's new to her. "Is everyone on the outside like you?"

The right answer to that one is probably "yes," and "no." I say nothing. The faces at the windows disappear. Someone is playing a flute. The man in the shiny black suit gathers

himself together. He gets up, steps toward me. The dog
waddles over behind him, stands quietly by his ankle. He
looks accusingly at Margo.

"You've told him nothing. You must have other things on
your mind." He turns to me, and I can see tears in his eyes.
"You've just arrived in New Jerusalem, and already you
don't know where you are." He takes a step backward, and
bows. He speaks again, and this time I feel I'm hearing a
speech he knows by heart, and says over and over.

"Along this alley are the death houses. In the slums of New
Jerusalem, where everyone who has a house or rents a
portion of a house has many tenants, it is only the owner or
sometimes the chief tenant, who finds it possible to die at
home. The sub-sub-tenants, who rent the stairway landings
and often the very steps themselves, have no room to die.
They go to this street of death houses.

"In each death house the first floor is for adult deaths.
The second floor is for infant deaths. These are short life
persons, and we are not interested in them. The same is true
for childless men and women. They have no one to truly
mourn them, so when they die, there is no importance to it.
Second floor. Do you understand now?"

I don't like his little story, and I throw it back at him.
"No...and it doesn't matter. I don't plan to die in New
Jerusalem." Margo is frightened, pulling me away from this
joker, and he's trying to scare me by grinning. We're
walking away, and he's shouting:

"Margo! Don't leave him! He's sure to get lost!"

Dr. Leroy's place is a group of low gray buildings surrounded by a barbed wire fence on three sides, the sea on the other. Manicured lawns. A sign reads: "NEW JERUSALEM LEPROSARIUM AND CLINIC FOR THE TREATMENT OF RARE DISEASES." As we approach the gate, I grab Margo's shoulders, and turn her to face me. It's still on my mind.

"Who was that guy back there?"

"Just a salesman," she says. With a quick twist of her body she wriggles out of my grip.

"He sells necklaces he lies about...and he allots places in the death houses."

"How come he spooked you?"

Margo snaps back. "Spooked? You don't step on a snake, that's all. You're a reporter, Faber. Just report. Don't go around New Jerusalem doing things."

"That's perfect. I suppose I just do what you or Runme Singh tells me."

"Just help me get this package, that's all. Then you can do whatever you goddamn please."

The New Jerusalem Leprosarium and Clinic for the Treatment of Rare Diseases specializes in maladies not yet diagnosed and classified by modern medicine. Each case is a medical first, and if the patient dies, the disease is named after him. If the patient is cured the disease is named after the doctor. This practice has given rise to abuse. Some of the destitute patients prefer immortality to cure, and deliberately refrain from taking their medication in the hope of a mention in the New Jerusalem Medical Record.

The chief of the institution is Dr. Leroy. The doctor is at

least six-four, so thin his skin stretches over the bones. He wears thick lensed glasses. Before they dropped him into New Jerusalem for malpractice, he was chief of therapeutic rehabilitation at Maple Run, a posh home away from home for lunatics with money.

Leroy leads us through the wards in his white suit, silver hair. Patients are busy with basketweaving, crayons, plasticene. Two lepers play checkers, silver fingers stack the dead by the ashtrays. Benson and Hedges Menthol. All patients in the leprosarium smoke them in deference to the doctor. His brand. A smuggled twenty year supply sits in a locked storage room.

Leroy asks his daily question to the dayroom.

"Is everybody happy?"

All the patients mumble back in the affirmative. Margo's staring at the ceiling, bored with the grand tour. The doctor doesn't care. It's the press he's focused on.

Black takes a double jump. "King me, damn you Parker!" yells one player. A train whistle obscures Parker's reply as he slaps a black checker on top of the one that's invaded his last row. The whistle fades, and I can hear the train approaching, somewhere nearby.

Dr. Leroy leans over the checker game, and explains to me how Parker made the checkerboard and checkers himself in the crafts shop.

"Took him months. Has a special meaning for him, that ugly little game. Now, if you'll step this way."

The train whistle rises again, and Dr. Leroy needs to shout to be heard. "Golden Blowpipe Express, New Jerusalem Railroad."

Dr. Leroy's office, a small room with windows looking out into the main wardroom. Margo lights a cigarette, crosses her legs. She puts on a pair of sunglasses, graduated gray, and sits very still. Maybe she's sleeping. It looks like we listen to him, until he decides we've listened enough, and then he'll go get whatever it is we've come for....

"Make sure your readers understand, Mr. Faber, that the human organism in its diseased state is something that the childish science of the West, and the ornate and bumbling superstition of the East have yet to deal with. Disease, Mr. Faber, is cure.

"A glance at you is enough." Leroy comes toward me, his nicotine-stained fingers probe my face. "Hold still!" He pulls down one eyelid, then inserts a finger into my mouth, pulls it out, wipes it off on his pants leg.

"The reddish tinge of your left cornea, whiteness on the tongue, a flaccidity of the neck muscles, a bit of heat in the center of the palm—these are to me like a highway sign would be to you. Billboards.

"If you stop thinking of your thoughts as localized in your brain, which organ is impervious to pain or disease, and think of them as they are, running amuck in the bloodstream, in the sympathetic nervous system, in the internal organs, you would begin, I say begin, to conceive of the question of health in another way altogether."

A man enters the rear door of the office, carrying a large white sack over one shoulder. Leroy turns, grabbing the man by his dirty shirt collar, drags him over in front of us. The man's eyes are as big as a St. Bernard's. He's sweating. Leroy holds the man at arm's length, not releasing his grip.

"Mr. Faber, the out-patient you see before you, my laundryman, as a matter of fact, is an excellent example. He has contracted a peculiar complaint. His perspiration, you will notice, is offensive, and similar to the stink of decaying fish. At this time every month he becomes morbidly restless and depressed. The laundry is done badly, or not at all. He wanders about the clinic grounds mumbling to himself about the behavior of the gods to men, and cursing them by name. He complains that being familiar only with dead people, the gods do not understand the living—himself in particular.

"This restlessness and depression can only be cured by his eating the flesh of dolphins. Before he came under my care, his neighbors would spy him, early in the mornings, coming up the alley to his hovel, a full grown fish on his back, dripping salt water and blood. They treated him with mingled disgust and awe. I'm not proud to say that the cure remains the same, but we administer it more discreetly. He is not a happy man, and when the craving is upon him he is wretched. The dolphin flesh is an absolute necessity, as fainting, dizziness, nausea, and nightmare appear and increase if the meal is not consumed.

"A curious case, don't you think?" says Doctor Leroy, as he shoves the bewildered laundryman out the door.

He moves closer to me and Margo. His pupils, beneath his thick glasses, seem to contract and expand in a regular rhythm. He speaks again, this time in a very loud stage whisper.

"The man is one of Big Tiny's failures, of course. Perhaps another of his sons, though he uses whatever infants he can find or steal. He feeds them the keph from the moment of birth, Mr. Faber, with an eyedropper into their tiny mouths. Mother's milk. He imagines that by thoroughly impregnating their bodies with the drug, he will create a human being with the power to lead his cult with miracles.

"Tiny is a fool, whispering his doctrines into the drugged ears of infants in the long nights. He puts the keph to work in minds not worth performing a lobotomy on. He force-feeds pearls to swine. Most of them die. Some become like the laundryman, not knowing which foot to put first unless they're told. I hear he has one now who's reached his fifth birthday, and shows possibilities. Of what, I don't know.

"In any case, as soon as the ship takes us all back outside, this Kamoro cult will receive a terminal jolt. The world will indisputably reveal to them that what they've believed all their lives is wrong. Most of them will probably flip very far out, and not come back.

"They don't keep up with the outside—a fatal mistake. Have you seen my library, Mr. Faber?" Dr. Leroy points to a pile of *Time* magazines, the most recent of them twenty years out of date, pages missing and torn. He picks up a stack of them in his arms.

"No one else on this island knows what's actually happening—but I do. The other world is my hobby, so to speak...."

Margo interrupts the doctor, in a very loud voice.

"Doctor Leroy—the package."

"Exactly," Leroy answers. He doesn't even glance at her.

"Mr. Faber, is there anything else you wish to know for your article?"

"Yes, doctor. What the hell is the keph?"

Sudden silence from the wardroom outside the office windows. The patients duck their heads, busy themselves as if someone has said a naughty word. Margo smiles, then grits her teeth to prevent herself from laughing at my stupidity. I just push on.

"Runme Singh told me a crazy fairy tale about a Kephiboy, spirits with sticks, and now you. . . ."

Leroy interrupts me. "Cult nonsense."

The doctor takes me over to the window that opens into the dayroom. "This is an interesting ignorance on your part, Mr. Faber." He points at a bald old man, looks Thai or Indian, his head bobbing aimlessly on his neck.

"See that patient, the one industriously attempting to open his can of plasticene? His name is Rasheed Ali ben Mohammed, and he claims to be the nine-hundred and thirty-fourth in a direct line from the Prophet. Some years ago he ran a little shop in New Jerusalem off the Rue du Loup. Each morning he stood in the backroom before a row of glass bottles. Each bottle was half-filled with a chemical and herbal concoction the color of milk. Behind him was a small fluid press, fitted with a draw spout at the bottom. He fitted the bottles to the spout, filled each with a viscous red liquid, and capped it. The room stunk of fish.

"Ali had been down to the beach that morning by five A.M. with his wagon. He picked up dolphin carcasses from the fishermen. Overcharged as usual. By six he had sold the carcasses for dog meat. By seven, he had one dolphin brain in the press, and the others in the cooler. The fish were getting rarer. If he got three a week toward the end, he was lucky.

"Rasheed Ali ben Mohammed was the world's only

manufacturer and purveyor of the keph, or dolphin brain extract. This was a profitable trade, and he had no rivals in it, as: dolphins are fast disappearing and no up-and-comer wants in to a dead-end trade; his list of preferred customers was large, and private—they'd deal with no one else; the secret of the drug's manufacture was his alone. He had killed the inventor, his elder brother, to get it—and it was therefore especially valuable to him. The business was his life.''

The press squeezes the last drop of fluid from the morning's three brains. Ali sits on a bench outside his shop, lights a White Owl panatella, watches the dawn. Three men in motley and dominoes come staggering around the corner, seem to be late night revellers from one of the more outré of New Jerusalem's nightspots, on their way home with a skinful. They are not. The first man grabs Ali's arms, twists them tight behind his back. The second man opens the door of the shop, and the first drags Ali inside. The third man is wearing cap and bells. He picks up Ali's lit cigar from where it falls on the ground, carries it carefully inside. He touches the glowing tip to Ali's eyelashes. They shrivel and burn. Then the eyes.

"The rest of this upsetting tale, Mr. Faber, is simple. They wanted the secret of keph manufacture. He did not tell them. They tortured him for a month, in every way your mind might imagine. It is not known whether they were agents of the Kamoro cult, or of the Tourist Promotion Board, independent entrepreneurs from the outside, or indeed, a group of patients from this very institution.''

Dr. Leroy forces a chuckle at his own final suggestion,

and he ends the tale. "In any case, they failed, but Ali was left as you see him. He is blind. He is no longer interested in the keph. He is interested in plasticene."

Leroy escorts us to his laboratory. Behind a lab table sits a tall blonde woman in a nurse's uniform, doing her nails. Frosty pink. I remember her from somewhere. Dr. Leroy leans back against the table, flexing and unflexing his fingers.

"Now, Mr. Faber, that you know some history, I will actually answer your question." Leroy taps his lab table with a glass rod—a lecturer impatient for silence. Margo lights another cigarette, wanders over to the far corner of the room, picks up a magazine. I may be the only pupil, but I'm paying attention.

"The keph or dolphin brain extract: an addictive drug, the secret of whose manufacture is now known to no one. It is a milky crimson liquid much the color and consistency of blood, or it can be dried to a light red powder, which on close examination can be seen to be crystalline.

"Neurological and cardiovascular effects—nil. It is solely a full spectrum brain stimulant, and functions only within the cerebral cortex. All attempts to analyze or synthesize have been unsuccessful. It can be absorbed through the skin, and this is the most common method of ingestion."

As Leroy talks, he perches himself up on the lab table, near his nurse. She smiles over at him like an approving mother, watching her child perform. He's excited now....

"The overpoweringly pleasant sensation the drug gives is most often described as the sensation of 'stopping' or 'waiting,' as if the worlds have suddenly ceased to turn, and you stand there, with total confidence they'll spin again, not caring if they do or they don't. Meanwhile, you can look around."

Dr. Leroy lies back on the lab table. His legs seem to be moving up and down all by themselves. His glasses fall off, hit the floor. His voice is raspy in his throat.

"On the streets of New Jerusalem, addicts are looked upon by non-addicts as degenerate scum. Non-addicts are looked upon by addicts as ignorant fools...." He raises his hands, palms his nurse's breasts through her white uniform, whispers to her, "They don't know the secrets of the deep like you and me, Janine."

Leroy has forgotten us altogether. He rubs his face between Janine's breasts. Her nail polish spills. Margo's had enough. She screams at him: "Dr. Leroy! The package!" Leroy jumps up, puts on his glasses, looks embarrassed. He bows to us from the waist.

"Wait here, please. I'll only be a moment." He disappears behind a door marked PRIVATE.

We wait. Janine hands me a magazine: *New Jerusalem, a Paradise for You*, another Tourist Promotion Board publication. A blurry black and white photo of Runme Singh, taken at least thirty years ago, graces the cover.

One hour later, Dr. Leroy has not returned. Margo has fallen asleep. Janine files her nails. She isn't looking my way.

I put down my copy of the *New Jerusalem, a Paradise For You*, and quietly open the door marked PRIVATE, and walk through, closing it behind me. I'm in a small operating room, skylight, walls lined with the cages of rats and rhesus monkeys. Someone has left the motor of the operating table running, and the chrome steel bed is rising slowly. Its hum blends with the tiny shrieks and squeals of the animals. No one home. I throw a switch and the table stops moving. Quiet. There's a fly somewhere.

I step through a beaded curtain at the far end of the room. Behind it is a narrow door. I open it. Bathroom—pink tile, cotton in jars, cans of every American spray deodorant. Dr. Leroy, in his white suit, lies in the center of the floor, looking up at me. One lens of his glasses is cracked and the pattern resembles a snail of some kind. His throat has been slit, the open edges of the wound turning dark purple.

I step back and close the bathroom door behind me. Runme won't get his package today. Somebody is in trouble, and it could be me. I look for another way out. Can't go past the nurse. . . .

The beaded curtain parts, and Margo steps in. She takes one look at me, opens the bathroom door. She doesn't even blink. Leaning over the corpse, she goes through the pockets, finally finding what she's looking for: a key.

"Let's get out of here," she says. "I don't like dead people." She takes my hand, leads me down a long corridor I had not seen before. Her fingers are smooth and cool.

We reach a gray door, unmarked, locked. Margo presses the key she took from Leroy's corpse into my palm.

"Lock it when you're done. I'll be downstairs in the reception area, reading a copy of *Loving Couples.* She takes out the magazine and shows it to me, as if to convince me she'll actually be there. Same issue I had on the plane. The cover features two women and a man. All three are naked and laughing, seated on a red plastic couch in a room I now realize looks very like the lobby of the Cockpit Hotel.

Margo whispers in my ear. "The package we're looking for is about the size of a shoebox. I saw it once from a distance. It's wrapped in newspaper and tied with string. You have about five minutes before the patients come looking for you."

She walks quickly off down the corridor. I unlock the door. It's a janitor's washroom, and the package is sitting in the open, above the sink, next to a can of Gre-solvent. I put the package under my arm, lock the door behind me. I walk rapidly down to the reception area. Margo stands up, tosses her magazine into a corner.

I can hear screaming from the wardroom. Nurse Janine bursts through the door, races by us in panic. The patient, Parker, is at her heels. Parker is sobbing, screeching as he clumsily runs after her: "Doctor! I want my doctor!"

Margo takes my free arm in hers. "Faber," she says, "lets get the hell out of here."

UP AT MARGO'S PLACE, AND AFTER

*...and then I loved thee
And show'd thee all the qualities o' the isle,
The fresh springs, brine pits, barren place and fertile....*
—Shakespeare, *The Tempest*

Margo's place, the penthouse of an apartment complex, was built in Arnheim's time as a deluxe hotel for the expanding tourist population. The elevator hasn't worked for twenty years. We walk up ten flights. Washing in the hallways, smell of piss, rotting vegetables. On the landings, half-naked beggars crowd together, motionless until we reach them. Then they stir, stretch out hands, shift slightly in their sleepy or drunken haze. We pass, and they sink back into stillness. On the eighth floor landing a family is cooking a small fish over an open fire. Smells good. They nod to Margo. I follow her on upstairs, the package tight under my arm. The hallway outside her apartment is littered with garbage, cigarette butts. Two teenagers lie in front of Margo's door, humping away in the dim light. Margo gets one foot under the girl's back, and rolls them over and away. She finds her key.

Margo's place: floor to ceiling windows on all four sides look out over New Jerusalem. It's spotlessly clean, containing only two pieces of furniture: a glass coffee table and a low bed in the center of the room. There's a tin stove made out of an old oil drum, basket of charcoal alongside it. Drawings of birds, fish, flowers—pen on rice paper—are tacked to a board in a corner. There's a mirror.

Margo shrugs out of the short jacket she's been wearing, throws it on the bed. She's got a sleeveless thing on underneath, leaves her thin arms bare. She claps her hands.

"Put the package down. We'll deliver it to Runme tomorrow." I hang onto it, and look at her. I've never wanted a woman more in my life, and I've got a feeling that if I let go of the package she'll disappear. I hold onto it. I ask the obvious question.

"What's in it?"

"Ask Runme Singh. It's his."

"Is he your father?"

She just looks at the floor. I go back to question one.

"What's in it?" Margo looks up at me, takes a deep breath.

"The keph, stupid. All that's left of it in New Jerusalem. You wanted to know, so I told you. Put it down."

Margo walks away from me, over to a window. She presses her nose against the glass. She takes a deep breath, exhales, and I can see her ribcage swell and then relax. She turns again to face me. I put the package down.

She kneels by the coffee table, centering the package on the glass as if it was posing for a still life and she was Cezanne. She pets the damn thing like it was a kitten. Outside her windows, night, and a bird lights on the windowledge. I can hear the beat of his wings in the air, hear him take one or two thin footsteps on the stone, and he's gone. Lights of the harbor below. Tiny silver pinwheels turn in the distant sky.

Margo's fingers dawdle over the string that ties the package shut, then draw away. She giggles. She goes into another room, comes back with a glass full of green liquid in her hand.

"Green Spot?"

"O.K." I take a long swallow, put the glass down, and her arms are around my neck, one of her thighs tight to my crotch, my hands on her ass. She throws her head back, and my mouth is on her neck, under her translucent ear, where a heavy black strand of hair curls and spirals. Blue lights of vidscreen replay flash through the scene. She smells like some other lifetime.

Her bed is soft and huge. Together we sink into it, and the heat of her is strange, a sensation of burning and of fever, like a baby rolling in disturbed sleep.

I'm coming in a minor blaze of glory, when a dead stranger knocks on the inside of my head—like a warning beeper, like a green cormorant throat full of fish and can't get it down, like a sudden physical blast of fatigue...and I push through it cockstrong to land on the far side, Margo's thigh on my palm, her ankle in my back, and I'm in her to the impossible hilt, her head thrown back like a sweaty medusa, and that wave breaks, and leaves me on the shore.

She rolls away from me and stands. She's being cute.

" 'Scuse me, Daddy, while I powder my nose.'' Her ass moves off toward the john. I pick the glass of Green Spot off the floor, take another sip, stand up. Feels good to be naked. I wander over to the window and look out—tiny circular lights of one ship, anchored in the center of the bay. Someone is singing somewhere, far off. It's a song I know, but cannot quite remember....

Then the room starts doing a twenty second fade into a red haze, and my knees buckle. I stumble back toward the bed. Margo is standing in the doorway, watching me fall. She has become much taller, and is much further away... another drunk done lost his shoes in this alley, not even strong enough to stand and why bother? Lie down and close eyes, everything be all right...package be all right...story be all right...little Faber be all right close eyes now till the strength come back like the elephant his trunk and the sun come up. Ooop! Lie down too hard! Don't wanna bump my nose before I sleep.

I never made it to the bed. I'm lying there on the floor, eyes stuck shut, head full of green jello, trying to fight whatever she slipped me in that drink, and losing. I can hear her voice through the fog, coming from a million miles away. Margo is talking to herself....

" 'Scuse me, Daddy, while I powder my nose...oldest story in the world....'' Footsteps going away, and then

back, close to my head, and I can smell her. I can't move.
Sound of a package being picked up, and then, being put
down. Her voice drifts, tangling in my head, words covered
with a gray film....

"Perfect match. One box for Runme—and this one in the
closet, under the lace underwear....He ain't getting none,
and Faber ain't getting none, and when that ship comes in,
the extract is gonna be in my suitcase, in a box marked
Chanel #5 bath powder. Ain't that right? Doesn't Margo
deserve the best, after living out her life on this scrap of shit
in the middle of some ocean? Give Runme the phony keph,
and before he finds out about it and can figure whether to
blame the switch on Faber, or Leroy, or whoever killed
Leroy, or me...by the time he's got it figured, we'll be in
the world again. I'll get so lost he'll never find me...."

The mickey wins, her voice is gone, and the world is a
sinking down, and darkness.

Cold wind. One half of my face is scraping concrete. Wet.
Blood. I open one eye. Still night. A hand is in my back
pocket, and it isn't mine. I roll over and grab a thin wrist.
Two yellow eyes shine out at me from the darkness. "Stop
hurt," says a voice like a frog's. I manage to get up on one
elbow, staring into what looks like a heap of rags about three
feet high. In the center is an old lady's face, brown like a
mummy, very tiny. Masses of blue veins stand out on her
forehead and neck. I try the classic.

"Where am I?"

"Nighttime," is the answer I get. She twitches pathetic-
ally, tries to free herself from my grip on her wrist. I hang
on tight to that skinny bone, look beyond her. Now I can

make out the ornate railing of the Bridge of Monkeys, two dancing baboons bathed in violet streetlight.

"Who are you?"

"Zuzu," says the bundle of rags. "Love money, chewing gum, rattles, picture books. Hate Chinamen, janitors, cold weather, people who try to be friendly. Zuzu thought you were dead. Look in your pockets for toys."

"Yeah." My head is clearing slowly. Somehow that bitch Margo must have had me dropped here. Side of my face is scraped raw, lump on my head. Everything else feels alright. My wallet's still there. I try to stand—can't make it. I figure I'll just lie here.

I let go of Zuzu's wrist, and then I spot a baby carriage behind her. It's stuffed with busted umbrellas, pieces of broken brick, scraps of clothing. A filthy teddy bear dangles off the pushbar. I crawl toward the carriage.

"Take me to the Cockpit Hotel. I give you money.... Money!" I wave my wallet under Zuzu's nose. The bundle of rags shifts, and her head blurts out into the light. Not a pretty sight.

"Unnnhhh," says Zuzu. I manage to climb into the baby carriage, legs hanging out, after a few disastrous tries. Zuzu stands, and I realize she's simply a dwarf lady, very old. It seems we got a deal, as she gets behind the pushbar, kicks up the brake. We roll.

I look up at the sky, tops of trees in dark silhouette move by. The bitch must have given me enough sleepytime to choke a horse. Where the hell's the package?...and I must have fallen asleep again. Next thing I remember is Zuzu shaking me awake outside the Cockpit Hotel. She holds out her hand, palm up. Morning. A sign hangs from the hotel's iron gates, written in black crayon on part of a brown paper bag. "HOTEL GONE TO AMERICA." The gate is open. The doorman and his stool have disappeared.

Inside, the lobby is empty. Near the registration desk the bellboy-bartender is busily doing something with his back to me. I come up quietly behind him, see him merrily stuffing the registration book, the brass gong, my other suit, my shaving cream, and my pistol into a plastic duffle bag.

I grab his shoulder, spin him around. Before I can say a word he panics, throwing his skinny body onto the floor at my feet, clutching the can of shaving cream to his chest. He's cursing me or begging my forgiveness in a language I don't understand, until I slap him hard across the face.

"Shut up," I tell him. "I'm not about to hurt you." He snaps out of it and stands up. He hands me the shaving cream, the pistol, and the wrinkled suit. He readjusts his turban on his oblong head. His little moustache is dripping sweat. He bows.

"Cockpit Hotel yours now, sahib. I give it to you. You be owner. Many rooms. Tourists be here soon. I come back tomorrow, teach you gin fizz, coco-loco. Very good for make drunk. Now you don't kill me when I walk away."

He begins to back toward the lobby exit doors, the red plastic duffle in his hands. I just look at him. He stops. "Oh, yes. Telegram, Mr. Faber." He takes a crumpled telegram out of his pocket. A piece of gum is stuck to it. He hands it to me, backs out the door. He waves goodbye.

I open the telegram. It's from my editor.

"FABER. WAITING FOR YOUR NEWS. THE SHIP HAS LEFT ITS PIER. SOON ALL OVER. REMEMBER. NEW

JERUSALEM ISNT THERE. WHATS THERE IS
YOUR STORY. LOVE AND KISSES. THE EDITOR."
     I crumple it up, throw it over my shoulder. What the hell
do I have to say? "Everybody's crazy here, and I don't know
what the hell's going on...?" I'll write the damndest story
he ever saw, the true story—when I got some idea what this
little world is all about. When I'm ready.

In the cocktail lounge of the abandoned hotel, Mr. Petersen
sits in an armchair, reading a yellowing copy of a newspaper.
The pages come apart in his hands. "Dateline—September
13, 1987." The year the island opened as a prison. The paper
must have come down tied to some parachuting criminal's
leg.
     Petersen sees me, lifts his glass in greeting. His eyes
glimmer in the neon light of the bar.
     "Le hotelier! Congratulations. I overheard your little
dialogue with our ex-bartender." I tell him I don't think it's
funny, and I can see he believes me. I sit down across from
him, light a cigarette. He looks somehow different than he
did on the plane, and then I notice it...a small black box
dangles from his neck, sits lightly on his belly, goes up and
down with his breathing.
     "You like it?" says Petersen. "I made it myself this
morning, out of two toothpaste boxes, a can of black Esquire
bootpolish.... I thought of gluing the fisheye for my Leica
to it—never use that lens anyway—but it would have been
too uppity. When in Rome, Faber...."
     Petersen pauses. At first I think he's gauging my reaction,
and then I can see he doesn't give a shit. He's got

something he's gonna tell me, and I can take it or leave it.

He takes a sip of his drink, leans back in his chair.

"Have you met Big Tiny? There's an interview. The man is quite amazing. Or have you been recruited by the other side?"

"What other side?"

"The Tourist Promotion Board," says Petersen. He gets up, goes behind the bar, and opens another Green Spot. I can see the back of his head in the bar mirror.

"Runme Singh," says Petersen. "He wouldn't pay his bill, you know. Laughed in my face."

"Didn't you steer me to Runme Singh in the first place? On the plane coming over?"

Petersen seems to find that funny. "Faber, a lot of people in New Jerusalem need favors right now—not just poor Runme Singh." He holds up his Green Spot. "This stuff tastes funny, but it grows on you. You try it?"

By this time I know an answer to that one. "Yeah. Not bad."

Petersen lowers his pudgy eyelids, considers me for a moment. "I'm bringing home an...approximate version of what's happening here. I don't know exactly what you've learned as yet, Faber, but I'd suggest you also be discreet in your dispatches. Let the world know too much—might be trouble later on."

"What kind of trouble?"

Petersen holds up his kamoro, puts it to his eye, lets it drop back into his lap. "Financial trouble," he says. "There are wonderful things on this island, Faber. Really quite amazing what Arnheim tried to do, and what's happened since. Kamoro cult, for example; one of those religions you laugh at—how could they be so stupid and all—and then, there it is. So simple. Do you understand?"

There's a long pause while Petersen studies me again, as if measuring me for some revelation yet to come. Silence between us. Finally Petersen looks me dead in the eye. Here it comes, whatever it is. The neon in the bar suddenly flickers, blinks out. A generator failed somewhere. Petersen pays no attention. His face is in shadow.

"Faber, don't be a fool. This little dying prison cum tourist trap turns out to be the goddamn motherlode. Let's be honest with each other. I hear you had a little talk with good Doctor Leroy before he died?"

I figure I better play it as dumb as possible. "Doctor Leroy?" I say to him, trying to get a blank expression onto my face. I must have succeeded. Petersen laughs.

"You're not an idiot, Faber. Please don't pretend with me. Yes, Doctor Leroy. I heard you killed him."

Looks like time for the deaf and dumb act is over.

"Bullshit," I tell him. "Whoever told you that lied."

"I didn't say I believed it. I said I heard it. The truth is, Mr. Faber, Leroy was trying to hold onto something that didn't belong to him. A lot of people would have killed him for it. Shoebox. You tried the keph yet, Faber?"

I shook my head. "No surprise," says Petersen. "None in circulation. Runme Singh figured the U.N. would close down the colony sooner or later, and he wanted a little something to remember it by. He used what remained of his power to buy or steal all the keph that was left in New Jerusalem. And he put it in a box.

"This box seems to be missing, and to compound the problem, there seem to be a number of phony versions of it floating about the island. It was supposedly in Leroy's drug safe at the clinic, and then it wasn't, and the doctor bit the dust."

"What's it worth?"

"Depends on what the traffic will bear, and once they've had a taste, the traffic will bear the weight of the pyramids. A little dab'll do ya, Faber. Enough in that box to addict North America quite conclusively. It can be cut a thousand to one and still be potent."

Petersen's hands make circles in the air in front of me. His tie stirs in a breeze from the overhead fan, twitches with a life of its own. He gives me a knowing look.

"Faber, you're an asshole. There's a good thing here, a once in a lifetime thing, and you're farting around. New Jerusalem isn't forever. Five days or so is a long way from forever. These people are convicts, children of convicts—all dumb enough to be caught. They can be taken. The keph is a hot item, and let me tell you the topper. They forgot how to make it. It's rumored that one guy knew the recipe, and he's a raving lunatic."

"I've heard something like that," I tell him. "Leroy gave me a lecture on the subject."

"Then you know that the stuff is as addictive as breathing. No side effects, no withdrawal pain, but you've got to have it, and you'll pay the price. Our price, Faber. Yours and mine."

Petersen takes a Minox camera out of his jacket pocket. He points it at me, and there's a barely audible click as he presses the shutter release.

"Abandoned Lounge of the Cockpit Hotel," says Petersen, in a bad imitation of a HomEnt newsbriefing. "Faber, a reporter for an American pseudo-news syndicate, polishes off the contents of the bottles left behind the bar in one gigantic zombie cocktail—his toast to the glories of New Jerusalem, now about to end forever!"

I stare at him. "You're gonna bring that photo to your paper?"

"Why not?" says Petersen. "They'll print anything, won't they? Think over what I told you. I'm going to bed. I've had a long night, Faber. Waiting up for you till dawn."

Mr. Petersen heads for the stairs, kindergarten Kamoro bouncing on his belly. Suddenly he stops, turns back to me.

"Flash!" he says. "New Jerusalem, five A.M." Now I'm sure Petersen's no longer playing with a full deck. He comes back toward me with a glint in his eye. "Before I go beddy-bye, let me give you a scoop. I have my sources. I wasn't there at the Bridge of Sand, mind you, but someone was. Someone sees everything in New Jerusalem.

"It seems that early this morning the woman purported to be Runme Singh's daughter, Margo, who I believe you've met, was striding rapidly over the bridge into Arnheim Lane—a package the size of a shoebox, wrapped in newspaper and tied with string, was under her arm. She was headed in the direction of Runme's house on Phoenix Road. Who knows if the box was genuine? My informant didn't get to poke his slippery fingers into the red dust. Leroy could have made a switch, so could Margo, and so could you.

"In any case, there goes Margo, with a delivery to make to Daddy, crossing the Bridge of Sand. Two men in business suits, with the instamatics of Kamoro cult obduratos strapped around their heads, grabbed her from behind. One ran his hands up under her sweater, tugged at her breasts in a mechanical way. Curiosity, really. Margo's quite the celebrity on the island. The other ripped the shoebox from under her arm. They pushed her down to the pavement. She scraped her palms. One of them kicked her in the small of the back. They disappeared. Whatever was in that box, Big Tiny's got it.

"Margo lay there, wondering, I imagine, what next. Then she stood up, continued the way she was going, up Arnheim Lane, into Phoenix Road.

"That's the news. I'm going to bed now. Think it over. You seem to be on the wrong side here."

"I'm not on any side."

"Then you're a fool, Mr. Faber. Goodnight, or rather, good morning. By the way, reporter to reporter—catch the volcano ceremony. I'll be there. Big Tiny's going to put on a little show at Mount Arnheim, in the center of the island. Day after tomorrow...though the boy won't be there, I don't think."

"The boy?"

"Big Tiny's son," says Petersen. "You should meet him. Give you a scare."

FILMING

In this island dwells three philosophers—
Suction the Epicurean, Quid the Cynic, &
Sipsop the Pythagorean. I call them by the
names of those sects, tho' the sects are not ever
mention'd there, as being quite out of date;
however, the things still remain, and the
vanities are the same.

William Blake,
An Island in The Moon

I wake up in the afternoon, head pounding. Time to tell
Runme Singh some story about how it all turned out, see if I
can get anything more out of him.

The town is quiet. Everyone must be home packing. I
reach One Phoenix Road, and it looks deserted. The broken
windows have been clumsily boarded over. I ring the bell. A
face appears at a window, then a guard unlocks, leads me
through to the sanctum sanctorum.

I wait for Runme. Armed guards still move in and out

with suitcases, cartons. Either Runme's got a helluva lot of souveniers, or the Kamoro cult has its points. I'm still trying to figure what to say about the last day and a half that he'll believe. I don't feel like speaking up about Margo's little games just yet. I want to get hold of her myself first. Besides, I hate telling stories where I'm the sucker.

Runme walks in, much more casual this time. No guards. He's decided he can trust me—or that I'm harmless. He come close, and I can see the man is scared to death. Two day stubble, bloodshot eyes, looks like he hasn't slept since I've last seen him. He seems about ten years older than he did the day before. His hair shows streaks of white, and his fingers shake as he fondles his medals. I take a good look at his chest, and realize again that anything from outside, understood or not, has value here.

   Runme's medals: a section of a Chef Boyardee Spaghetti-Os can, square inch pounded flat showing the chef's face and part of his toque blanche; a New Jerusalem Tourist Promotion Board Official Guide pin with a large number one on it in gold; an old Deputy Sheriff's badge out of a Post Toasties box; a pin with a faded picture of the 1970s rock star Elvis Presley on it. This one says around the rim: "Elvis Will Never Die."

I didn't need to worry about my story. Rumme seems to be much better informed about the incidents than I am.

   "You didn't kill Dr. Leroy, did you?" he asks, patting my shoulder in a friendly way.

"He's dead?" I say, hoping I don't sound too phony. "He was fine when we left him."

Runme laughs. "I'm glad to know, Mr. Faber, that men from the outside lie as well. Even reporters. Or perhaps you've been infected by the City of New Jerusalem. Your lies are refreshing, Mr. Faber," says Rumme, "but dumb. They do not help us. She stole it from you, didn't she? She came here, told me lies about the Kamoros stealing it from her. But, you must realize, Faber, that very package I sent you for may have been only a facsimile itself. Leroy was a devious creature. So is the lovely Margo. It's the effect of the island, the company one is forced to keep. She was an angel child—a bubble of joy—and then she absorbed her mocking ways like a virus. If you are her lover now, Mr. Faber, I envy you—and I pity you."

Runme pauses, lost in his own thoughts. I don't seem to have anything to say. Then Runme gathers himself, and comes on with a new surge of geniality.

"There's no need, Mr. Faber, for our relationship to flounder on the misadventures of last night. We have other possibilities. Do you know Sir Rodney Blessington?"

"We met at my hotel. He told me some things about the island."

"Very informative, I'm sure. Sir Rodney has quite the individual perspective. In any case, I've given him a little commission to carry out for me, in connection with another possible location of my package. Yet he is not completely trustworthy—if you understand me. It would be in my interest, and in yours as well, of course, if he should carry out this commission without any slipups."

Runme takes the time to refresh my memory about the

carrot I'd jumped at. "A newspaper of your own, Faber! A man like you shouldn't be chasing around godforsaken islands in the hope of a byline.

"New Jerusalem time is running out. McPeak, at the airport communications building, has begun to receive signals. I hear the Santa Maria's arriving in three days from now."

"The Santa Maria?"

"McPeak's nickname for the ship."

I bother to fill him in. "The ship's the United Nations Hospital Transport 'Florence Nightingale.' Used to be a cruise ship. It was the only liner big enough to carry you all. Its got fifty shuffleboard courts."

"Shuffleboard?" says Runme.

I don't bother to explain that one. Instead, I tell him Petersen's story about Margo being mugged for the package by two Kamoro cult members. Runme nods.

"She told me the same tale. It might even be true. What she neglected to tell me was what was in the package. Perhaps she didn't know. Whatever she had, Big Tiny probably has it, so where we once prayed for that particular box to be genuine, let us now as fervently wish it to be filled with shit.

"But enough of these complications. See Sir Rodney. Tell him to take you along tomorrow evening. You might interview him as well. He's our premier artiste here in New Jerusalem, since Arnheim's death."

Runme Singh is dreaming of the girls in the porno magazines of his youth, and he knows he has to buy them soon or never. Here in New Jerusalem he's a beleaguered and ineffectual dictator. In America he'll be a bum with a record unless he comes away with something. The only thing in New Jerusalem to come away with is the keph. I feel a little pity for him—but not much. And I don't believe his promises. Mainly, I want to see what happens.

"I'll go," I say. "Where do I find Sir Rodney?"

"He'll be out near the Masquerade tomorrow afternoon, filming one of his epics." Runme beckons me over so he can whisper to me. His lips move soundlessly a moment before he speaks. He smells of cheap perfume.

"Kamoros everywhere. Insane. No need to fear if you use your head. Use your head." He touches his own head, then mine, with one finger.

"Sir Rodney does it anyway. I respect that, Faber. He didn't go Kamoro. Not Sir Rodney. Does it anyway."

"Does what?" I ask him.

"Filming. No film. No film on the island for twenty years."

On the outskirts of the city of New Jerusalem there are giant dioramas in which lifesize clockwork figures performed their parts in obscure dramas Arnheim designed. There were originally four of these, placed at the points of the compass, but there is only one in working order. The others were stripped during the chaos, and parts of the figures serve as display mannequins or signboards for shops in the various quarters of New Jerusalem.

The four dioramas are titled: NORTH-WORK AND PLAY, EAST-THE FATE OF THE FAMILY, SOUTH-DURING THE MONSOON, WEST-THE MASQUERADE.

I head west, walking a dirt road out of town, occasional
shacks, brown patches of garden. Hot sun on my back—and
then I see it, a portion of the landscape cut off from the rest,
sitting there in its own light and time.

It is a field at dawn, covered with snow and ringed with
willow trees. There are six figures in the scheme, in two
groups. In the center of the field is a dying Pierrot, lying on
the snow with a small red wound at his breast. Blood pumps
out of the wound in a garish, uneven spray, as if the
mechanism that controls it is faulty. Around him are three
other figures, all of which bob up and down from the waist
around the motionless white clown. The figures are worn,
and portions of their costuming have been stripped away.
One is dressed as a doctor of the time of Marco Polo, and he
holds a surgical probe in one hand. Another figure is in a
ruffled neckpiece and high boots, and he holds an empty
velvet-lined box. The third figure is bearded, in a black robe,
perhaps that of a monk of some order unknown to me.

Walking away, at some distance from the central tableau,
are a dancing figure in motley, and another dressed as an
Iroquois brave, feathers and a shawl. Someone has slung a
cardboard kamoro around this figure's neck. These two
move toward the artificial horizon in a slow gliding motion.

Far off, at the very edge of the field, other figures can be
dimly seen, women perhaps. It is always dawn, circular
diorama of a snow-covered field, ringed with willow
trees....

I hear voices from beyond the backscreen of the "Masquerade." I circle till I can walk behind the giant cyclorama.
From the back, a different show. The painted canvas is held

up with rotting two-by-fours, graffitti on the back—pornographic doodlings, one old crude drawing of a dolphin in a cage on wheels.

About a hundred yards beyond there's a stone quarry. Men and equipment, little figures in the distance. It feels like about 102 in the shade. My shirt is stuck to my back. I pull off my suit jacket, throw it over my shoulder, loosen my tie. I walk toward them.

Sir Rodney and his crew are famous in New Jerusalem: the anemic Wiggins, Roderick Kine and Bill Swerve, the grips and gofers, all living out of Sir Rodney's pocket, drunk and surly to everyone but him...and Miyoko Yakimoto, his lover, scriptgirl, and sometime actress. Miyoko is about forty, with some gray in her black hair, worn very long to her waist. She wears a deep red cheongsam and dark glasses.

They are currently filming the Tourist Promotion Board's version of the history of New Jerusalem for the British Museum archives. Sir Rodney has hired the delightful Miss Yakimoto to perform a leading role. She's on salary. The other performers are recruited on a day to day basis. Sir Rodney signs them to ornate contracts giving them large percentages of the film's eventual profits in lieu of cash down. What he delivers during shooting is a bottle a day and a place to sleep it off. Realism is Sir Rodney's forte.

Sir Rodney Blessington is a ferocious, unselfconscious parody of himself: ascot, moustache, sunken chest, jodpurs, very high bootheels. At the moment he is shoving about the arms, legs, and heads of his extras, setting them up as carefully as a window dresser, posing them against the quarry wall. They look like a crowd recruited from the men's shelter. Some of them can barely stand. They're dressed in exaggerated guerilla fighter oufits: berets, false beards, phony armslings, camouflage suits.

I figure I'll catch Sir Rodney between takes. I sit down to watch the show. Sir Rodney takes a step back, looks over the setup. He addresses the cast.

"Remember, you raggedy bastards, you're in show business. This film will make history. I want you to die gloriously. You are patriots!"

Sir Rodney's arms swing wide as he indicates himself, his cameraman, grips, and Miss Miyoko Yakimoto on sound for the moment. "Think of us," he says, "as the firing squad. When those bullets hit on the soundtrack, I want to see your humanity. I want to see the vulnerability of heroes. When you go down, like babies under the strap!"

"Sir Rodney!" his cameraman interrupts. "Pssst!" The cameraman has an old Bell and Howell on a tall wooden tripod. He and his camera are perched on top of Sir Rodney's '61 Rolls. Sir Rodney cocks an ear in his direction.

"Bloody bastards can't understand you, you know. None of that lot speak the English."

Sir Rodney isn't fazed by the news. "Just going through the proper formalities, Wiggins. I don't want anyone saying I didn't direct this picture. Besides, these people understand me, in their way."

Sir Rodney turns again to his cast.

"Patriots, ready!" He turns to his crew.

"Ready? Roll sound!"

Miyoko presses the start button on a cheap cassette recorder.

"Camera!"

Wiggins, on the car roof, flips on the old Bell and Howell, points it at the ragged line.

"ACTION!"

The extras begin some amazingly bad death scenes. Then the side door of Sir Rodney's Rolls slides open, revealing a Ghurka machine-gunner hunched over a Gatling gun. He is covered in cartridges. Bubbles of pink froth edge Sir Rodney's lips, and his moustache wiggles.

"FIRE!"

The sound is like a dull cough over and over as the gunner opens up. The quarry reeks of blood. Sir Rodney screams: "CUT!"

One body is still moving, a man in a steel helmet and camouflage shorts, curling up like a fetus, holding his belly. Then he's still. Sir Rodney is not pleased with the take. He looks up at Wiggins.

"They couldn't act anyway. Ah, well...tomorrow's another day, lad. Now how about a tall cool one at the Octopus Lounge?"

They begin to pack their filming gear into the car. I keep thinking it's got to have been some kind of stunt, the magic of movies. I get up my nerve, walk casually over to the quarry wall. No one pays any attention to me. The bodies are very real—and very dead.

I look over at Sir Rodney and his ludicrous crew, and it's hard to believe that these people are not only dangerous—they're criminally insane. Their only concerns about the event are artistic ones. They're people who stage auto accidents, then complain that the victim's blood is too dark to contrast properly with the blacktop.

I try to get a word in, but Sir Rodney is too creatively involved, or too stoned. He doesn't seem to remember me from the hotel. That Runme Singh sent me also draws a blank. Meanwhile, the rest of the crew have packed the car so full of equipment that only Wiggins, the driver can fit in. He pulls away, and the grips start walking. As Sir Rodney begins to stroll off, he calls back to me over his shoulder.

"Faber, is it? Later, at the Octopus."

He's gone over the hill, tapping his calf with his riding crop. Miyoko, however, remains. She likes the press—drawn by the old notebook like a fly to sugar. She's a good interview....

"I'm a Shiatsu School dropout, so I know where to press, honey. My mother was born in Hiroshima on bomb day, and I still write letters to the caretaker at the cemetery where Harry Truman's buried, ask him to lay the letters on Harry's grave."

"How come," says I, and Miyoko tells me how she got her natural advantages.

"The bomb blew, and Mom slid outta grandma's belly and into the doctor's hands. The two of them were fried. She lived. She had me. I got the blast in every cell. I got so much mutation even the mutations are mutating. Under a microscope, I sizzle."

"Tell me something about Sir Rodney," I ask, and Miyoko speaks right up. Not the kind of information I was hoping for, but interesting....

"Sir Rodney is only able to achieve erection in unfamiliar

surroundings: a hotel room, the home of a casual acquaintance, airplanes, terminals, restaurants. This difficulty necessitates frequent changes of living quarters. Sir Rodney is difficult to find. Often his own film crew cannot locate him for days."

"Where's the Octopus?"

But Miyoko's had her fun, and she's already walking away, toward Sir Rodney, the top of whose head is just disappearing behind a hill. She runs.

I sit in the Octopus Lounge, a cocktail bar on a corner of Phoenix Road, near the Bridge of Teeth, overlooking the Plaza del Cocodrillo. Seediest part of New Jerusalem: arcades, street vendors slumming for the elite, whores in leopard skin bathing suits. Occasionally they stroll by the window, point between their legs and stick out their tongues.

A neon octopus over the bar blinks its red eye. It feels like I've been here forever. I'm waiting, and Margo won't stay out of my mind. Her face is drifting through everything—dragging up in me all of my feelings at once—and I sit with them, hopelessly trying to sort them out....

At last, near midnight, Sir Rodney enters with his entire crew. Miyoko spots me, leads them over to my table. I'm surrounded. Wiggins points his camera at me. Sir Rodney looks vague.

Partial Transcript of My Interview With Sir Rodney Blessington:

SIR RODNEY: I'm Sir Rodney Blessington, the filmmaker. Who are you?

FABER: I'm Faber, remember—the reporter who was sup-
posed to meet you here.
SIR RODNEY: The reporter!
FABER: We made this meeting this afternoon, outside of
town.
SIR RODNEY: This is too embarrassing. *I* suggested *this*
place as the location of an interview?
FABER (thinking that I never said a word about inter-
viewing him): Yeah. I never heard of it before.
SIR RODNEY: My god! I'm ruined.

At this point I figure I better lay it on thick if I'm going to
get any sense at all out of this madman. I was ready, did my
research that afternoon. Sir Rodney had been the last of the
great Hollywood decadents. When they wouldn't buy it for
him anymore, because he wasn't worth it anymore, he
began to buy it for himself. Only Sir Rodney didn't have
enough money to buy it for himself. No one does. He began
to steal. They caught him, and the next thing he saw was the
rooftops of New Jerusalem between his shoetops as he
floated down.

FABER: Sir Rodney, I'm one of those who have found
meaning for my life in your later films. *Balkan Rhapsody*,
Rainbow of Hell, *The History of New Jerusalem* . . . I know
them all.
SIR RODNEY: Mr. Faber, I wonder if you realize that your
statement is particularly interesting in view of the fact that
Balkan Rhapsody has received exactly two theatrical show-
ings, at 8 and 10 one evening in a basement club here in
New Jerusalem. Twenty years ago. For the 10 o'clock
showing we had a good crowd. However, the projector bulb

blew. No spare. At the 8 o'clock showing all went well. Three people were present, and I recall every face. You were not among them.

The one extant print of *Rainbow of Hell*, made before my unfortunate incarceration, was sold to a collector of the unusual at an enormous sum.

As for *The History of New Jerusalem*, that is only a very tentative title for the film I am shooting now....

FABER: Psychic, ain't I?

SIR RODNEY: What exactly do you want?

FABER: Just a decent story. What does every reporter want?

I mention softly that Runme Singh thought our meeting might be a good idea. Sir Rodney sobers up. He jars forward like a puppet, finger to his lips. A gesture, and his crew is gone. Sir Rodney leans over the table toward me, his right eye bulging from its socket. I tell him Runme's suggestion. He rubs his palms against the damp tabletop in a circular motion.

SIR RODNEY: It's true, Faber, that I have a rather delicate business transaction to undertake for Mr. Singh tomorrow evening. I agree that it would be excellent if you'd accompany me, and we could continue this pleasant conversation on the ferry. I plan to be paddled out to a certain ship in the harbor. I hope this won't inconvenience you. It's true that a witness to these negotiations, someone impartial who could testify that I carried out my commission, would be quite valuable....

Sucker time. Sir Rodney is too eager to have me around.

He needs me for something, probably to point at in the
line-up, if necessary. But I figure, keep my eyes open and
my hands in my own pockets and I'll be all right. Might be a
good story angle. Might be more.

   Sir Rodney stands, and smiles.

SIR RODNEY: Meet me tomorrow, midnight, pier seven, at
the harbor.

TO THE VOLCANO

> *When the leper woman gives birth to a child*
> *in the dead of night, she rushes to fetch a torch*
> *and examine it, trembling with terror lest it*
> *look like herself.*
> —Chuang Tze, trans. Burton Watson

An endless line of men, women, and children, heading up along the dusty dirt path to the rim of Mount Arnheim, the island's only active volcano. As usual in a New Jerusalem crowd, every race and nationality conceivable is represented. They're dressed in faded Hawaiian shirts, bermuda shorts, golf hats, sunglasses, airline baggage tags, travel stickers, fragments of knapsacks...all with the black boxes of the Kamoro cult hung around their necks or tied tightly to their faces, so that the small square hole cut into the box is their only avenue of vision.

At the head of the line is Big Tiny, a vintage instamatic strapped around his skull, one eye to the viewfinder. He is a huge man wearing a torn airline pilot's hat, a shirt printed with hula girls and surf-boarders, and plaid bermudas. In his arms, held out in front of him like an offering, is the package the cult stole from Margo. They are marching; I'm marching with them. Your reporter, bringing you the play by play.

There's some dancing and chanting, but most are quiet, or they mumble in low voices: "Magnavox...Motorola...." I look for familiar faces among the marchers, spotting the janitor I met cleaning out the government office...and toward the rear of the line, Harry the Horse. Harry walks in silence, dead blue eyes staring up at the volcano. I'm walking a few paces behind him, and I notice his attention shift from the volcano ahead to the crowd. He eyes them like a cop on the beat. Maybe Harry is some kind of bodyguard for Big Tiny, making sure that no lunatics trouble the calm sanity of his followers.

We've left the city of New Jerusalem far behind. The cult has been marching all morning and into the afternoon without a stop, landscape dry, the sky a very clear blue. The heat is intense. The Kamoro cult members refuse to talk to the press or to just a guy named Faber who wants to know what the hell's going on.

Big Tiny is surrounded by followers, and a good ways ahead of me. No chance to get through to him. Some sort of major ritual is in progress, but if anyone except Big Tiny knows what happens when we reach the volcano, they're not telling me. The rim of the crater is about a mile from the head of the column now, and the going's gotten steep. A dull hiss as steam escapes from rocky vents in the earth around us, and the air above the crater itself dances and shimmers with the heat rising from below. A thin plume of fire leaps suddenly from the crater, falls back into it in a lazy red arc, like a tiny skyrocket.

A man comes out of the crowd toward me. It takes a moment, and I recognize Petersen. He's either gone completely Kamoro, or he's faking it. The black box he showed me at the hotel hangs around his neck. His chubby white legs stick out from a pair of patched seersucker bermudas, baby-blue. A T-shirt, some sizes too small, is stretched across his belly. On it are the words: "Surf's Up." Petersen is sweating from the climb, but he's in an expansive mood. He throws one arm around my neck.

"Faber," he says, "glad you made it. Listen—the script here is for Big Tiny to destroy the box of keph in the cleansing fires, so that Runme Singh and the devils of the Tourist Promotion Board will be unable to steal it back— and use it to buy away all the treasures from outside these people believe are being sent to them by their gods on the incoming ship.

"That's what they actually believe the ship is, Faber. A load of all the modern goodies they've only dreamed of, or dimly remember. Dumb, eh? Especially throwing a billion dollars worth of keph into a hot hole?

"Tiny's not dumb. He's a wise man, Faber. You can't tell the people everything. Even Jesus didn't tell the people everything. He was careful. Tiny's careful. You see Tiny's head? You see it, Faber?"

I look up toward the front of the line, try to locate the tallest of the bobbing dark spots. Petersen keeps talking.

"Full of visions. Tourists fly through that head like clouds of migratory birds. In his vision of appliances, they're all

wrapped like Christmas gifts when he was four years old.
They shine like bumpers fresh from the car wash. Tiny is an
obdurato—one of those in the cult who never removes the
kamoro from his head. He's a man who's seen the world
through the viewfinder of a kodak instamatic for ten years.

"You know what he's doing right now? Like all the
obduratos, he's learned to frame to his taste. World's
greatest photographers, but they never take a picture. Do
you understand that, Faber? Right now, Tiny has the
shoulder and part of the back of the head of the marcher in
front of him foreground right, the volcano in the distance,
and a mental subtitle on which he focuses...TO THE
VOLCANO. He knows what film he's in. You understand
that, Faber? *His* film."

I try needling Petersen a little. "Looks to me like Big
Tiny's got a narrow view of things."

Petersen doesn't see the humor. "You don't understand,
and it doesn't matter. You don't have to. Good-bye, Faber.
I'll find you again before the ceremony."

Petersen disappears into the marching crowd. Now that
they've seen me talking to Petersen, the cult members near
me open up. I manage to get a few legends of Big Tiny's rise
to leadership, and some doctrine besides.

Early on in his career as a cult leader, Big Tiny taught his
cat and his parrot to drink from the same dish. He displayed
this achievement publicly in front of the government center.
He believed that he had brought about the millenium. This
belief was soon shattered by the god Betamax, who assumed
the shape of a popular film actress from the outside, in order
to lure him from these fruitless studies.

A practice Big Tiny encourages is the ritual followed for requests from the gods. Rain, for example. At first, a believing citizen of New Jerusalem simply fastens over his door a strip of paper, on which is printed the image of the god in charge of rain. If heaven proves dead to this supplication, a procession is organized in which an immense statue of the god, made of wood and paper, is carried about in a circle to music. If the god still will not give rain, prayers are changed to curses, the statue is ripped to pieces, and the god is insulted, reviled, spit, and pissed upon until the clouds gather and the first drops are felt by his worshippers. This particular ritual, according to my sources, has never been known to fail.

Big Tiny also teaches that there is a bird of paradise living in the air above the island of New Jerusalem. It was born among the clouds when the island began, and there it remains, drinking fog and eating mist. It will never touch the earth until it dies, whereupon it will fall heavily to the ground.

We approach the volcano's rim. I scrabble up toward the head of the line to get a better view of the action. It's steep here, bare rock and black dirt, some of the rock hot under my hands. I climb, starting little avalanches, stones flying away from my feet. I get within thirty yards of Big Tiny, settle myself on an outcropping of rock with a good view of the rim itself. The glare of the superheated air is intense, hot cinders flying. Then I feel a hand on my shoulder. Petersen squats alongside me. We look up together at the crater of Mount Arnheim.

Big Tiny walks majestically forward, alone, the package held out before him. Silence from the cult members. Tiny moves slowly, taking his time. He's only a few yards from the rim now. I'm looking, and Petersen's voice is the soundtrack.

"Here's how Big Tiny figures this one. Under his robe he's got a package, exactly like the one he carries, but filled with sand from the seashore. It's there as a possibility. If temptation proves too strong, Big Tiny wants to be sure he's got the means to succumb. The switch is no problem. He's going up to the lip of the volcano all alone. Believe me, Faber, if Big Tiny tosses a box into Mount Arnheim—it's not the keph."

Big Tiny on the edge. He stares into the glow of Mount Arnheim through his viewfinder. The hairs on his arms begins to whiten at the tip, shrivel, and burn. From my angle, I can spot him poking a hole in the package stolen from Margo. Final check. He curves his back toward the crowd, licks a finger, sticks it in the hole. It comes out covered with red dust. Tiny's eyes light up. He rubs it on the inside of his wrist. He's sensing inside himself now, and he's drawing a blank. Something's wrong. He brings his finger to his nose, sniffs. His nose wrinkles in disgust. I know what he's got. Margo's Chanel #5 bath powder. Tiny is furious, his face torn with anger and disappointment. He don't got it, and what's worse, he thinks he knows who does. He curses Runme Singh under his breath. Religion and greed boil together in his head.

Big Tiny suddenly throws the package high, leaving his arms frozen at the top of the swing. The grand gesture—and as the package falls into the volcano's depths, a great sigh sweeps the crowd. Big Tiny keeps his phony box tight under his robe. No need for it.

The sun is setting now, cut in half by the sea. The crowd begins to break up, head back downhill. Big Tiny beckons, and Harry the Horse weaves his way up through the mob. They're together, and Big Tiny bends over toward Harry's ear. Harry is expecting a whisper, and jerks his head back quickly. I hear Tiny clear, even at this distance. He's screaming. "Runme Singh! Runme Singh!" His face is a mask of fury. A cloud of hot ash rises from the crater, and a sudden breeze swirls black dust around their huddled forms. Tiny talks, Harry listens, but I can no longer hear them. A last weak flare of red fire streaks up into the twilight. Action's over for now. The worshippers go home. I'm still out on the street. I got a late appointment, at the harbor.

I'm down onto level ground. Stray bits of neon begin to light along the city's skyline a few miles away. Looks like some of the generators in New Jerusalem haven't yet been stripped for parts and stuffed in suitcases. I came this way in company, going back alone. Everyone has either disappeared or knows a shortcut back to town.

Empty road, no moon. Then ahead of me I spot a man's silhouette, black on black. It doesn't move. I'm getting closer now, and it's still motionless, like a cardboard cutout of a man set in the road. I stop. We both stand there, if he's real. A voice echoes in the darkness.

"Scared you, didn't I?" Petersen. I walk up to him.

"Yeah, you scared me."

Petersen's kamoro dangles from one hand. In his other is

a small automatic pistol. He slips it into a pocket of his bermudas.

"You're not the only frightened man in New Jerusalem, Faber. Another moment and I would have shot you." And I'm telling myself, Faber you're an asshole to walk around this town without your own gun—damn thing's heavy, and I leave it behind. No more.

Petersen takes my arm, like this is the Champs Elysée, and we walk toward town. He laughs. "Caption!" he says, in a very loud voice. "Two American Reporters Walk in Darkness in New Jerusalem." And then his tone changes.

"Listen, Faber. Have you decided?"

I play cute. "Decided what?"

"Whether to be rich. Your end is Runme Singh and his associates—my end, Big Tiny and his people. One of us is going to find that box of keph. We split, down the middle."

Petersen smiles, tightens his grip on my arm. "I hate spelling these things out, Faber. It all seems so melodramatic that way. But you force me."

We're walking, and the city is getting closer, and I'm thinking. Like everyone I've run into in New Jerusalem, Petersen seems a bit untrustworthy, to say the least. I've been running the only honest game in town. The chances of him sharing anything with your reporter seem about a thousand to one. Then again, maybe I should try to grab the damn box for myself. I could use some spare change, buy a thing or two. . . .

All this buzzed through my head, leaving me with only one thing clear. I didn't want to get involved with Petersen. I tell him so, knowing he has only one way to understand that from his angle—that I was going after it all myself. I wasn't sure I wasn't, and I didn't bother to change his mind. He lets go of my arm, stops walking.

"Then we part company here, Mr. Faber. But our paths are unlikely to run parallel or diverge."

I walked away from him, my back twitching till I was about a hundred yards down the road. I listened for all I was worth, not turning my head. Not a sound. When I finally looked back, the moon was up, and the road behind me was empty.

DEALINGS ON
THE WATER

*....and sorcerers, and idolators, and all liars,
shall have their part in the lake which
burneth with fire and brimstone: which is the
second death.*

—Revelation 21:8

The city of New Jerusalem hops like a tethered humming-
bird. The sun has set hours ago, and the heat is still
overpowering. Along the docks, in the narrow area between
the piers themselves and the warehouse godowns, men are
gathered in small groups, eating out of wooden bowls which
they wipe clean with their shirttails. Tied up along the
wharves are junks, sampans, old Chris-craft inboards, an
antique U.S. Coast Guard destroyer fitted over as a nightclub. Black barges with panels of corrugated sheet iron
roofing them over, torches lit at the prows, glide slowly past
the piers. These barges carry rice husks, sawdust, charcoal,

green bananas—whatever else has been made, grown, or
delivered up by the sea.

A butcher stands in the tail of his pigboat like a Venetian
gondolier; a pig's head is nailed to the prow, the rest of the
carcass laid out in the anatomically correct order down the
length of the boat. The curled tail is nailed to the stern. The
pig has been expanded, so to speak, and set out for sale.

I find the ferry pier. Sir Rodney stands at the far end, his
back to me, looking out over the water. As I walk up behind
him, a great Arab dhow glides by, almost touching the pier
end, great banks of oars sweeping the oily water. The whip
of the overseer cracks as he lashes the rowers, and the echo
skims out over the bay. I can hear the oarsmen chanting as
the dhow pulls out toward the open sea. Sound fades,
mingles with the scurrying of water rats.

Sir Rodney is lost in a melodramatic version of thought
with a capital T. I lean against the railing a few yards down
from him, look out for the incoming ferry. A mist is on the
water, and the few lights still visible out on the bay have
turned bluish and indistinct.

Click of high heels behind me. Coming down the pier
with her red dress on, Miyoko Yakimoto, the fizz-bang girl.
Another passssenger on this little cruise. She nods to me,
slips off her dark glasses. I turn back toward the water, and
then Miyoko slides up behind me and runs her tongue
around the inside of my ear. She wraps her arms around my
waist and holds on, tight and quiet. Sir Rodney still stares
out to sea, distracted. His fingers twitch behind his back,
and he locks them, squeezing them together to stop their
motion. He's reciting a poem under his breath: "If you can

keep your head when all about you are losing theirs. . . ."
He sweats.

Miyoko's tiny breasts slide up and down my back, and she whispers in my ear.

"Mr. Reporter, follow this closely, please, and remember me when we get to America. Sir Rodney is a genius. He needs money. The keph is free. You must understand that. Anyone who says they own it is a liar.

"Runme Singh suspects that Dr. Leroy, intending to steal the real package, sent it off to a safe place and replaced it with a facsimile. It is well known that the pirate, Wu Fang, often intercepts objects on their way to a safe place. We will take the ferry out to Wu's ship, the Black Bastard. Runme has engaged Sir Rodney to discover if Wu Fang has it, and if he has it, to buy it with the money Runme's given us.

"Once we've got it, Sir Rodney intends to substitute a facsimile, give that to Runme, and sell the real thing on the mainland to the highest bidder. Do you understand now?"

Miyoko lets go of me. Sir Rodney turns and looks at us, with a hopeless expression on his face, as if to say it's a world of thieves, and we have to live in it. He's been listening. He strokes his moustache.

"There's no real need," says Sir Rodney, "for me to expose myself to Runme Singh's wrath through the duplicity Miyoko attributes to me. The proprietor of our Tourist Promotion Board has already promised me a healthy cut. . . enough to finance a few independent productions. And Faber, there's no need for your report to Runme to include her babble. I'm well able to make it worth your while to slide over into the realm of artifice in this matter."

He turns away, begins to check the faded bundle of pesos,

yen, dollars that Runme slipped him, probably doping out
how much he can hold out for himself and still make the
buy.

"Ars longa, vita brevis," says Sir Rodney Blessington to
the air. Miyoko fingers a nerve at the base of my spine, then
another. The good feeling goes everywhere. The ferry
comes out of the mist, and Sir Rodney quivers, stares at the
swaying lantern on its prow.

The ferry is a flat wooden raft with a lantern hung on a pole
at one end, and a sweep oar and a ferryman at the other. The
ferryman is in rags, and is silent. We slide away from the
pier in even strokes, the three of us sitting huddled together
in the raft's center, the ferryman looming over us, his
bearded face blue in the lantern glow. The night is blacker
than hell, and the mist is fat and heavy, moving in waves off
the warm bay. It takes us into itself, till we four become
haloed ghosts shimmering in the lantern light. Water slaps
the sides. A buoy clangs. Sir Rodney is twitchy. Miyoko is
calm. I feel like we're getting lost forever. There's nothing
out there and we're heading right for it....

Then, a low, steady voice from behind me.

"Now just cause I'm the ferryman don't mean I got a
story to tell you...but I do. Daddy told it to me in the reeds
before I was born.

"When it all started, earth and heaven were floating
everywhere in little pieces. Then my grandfather showed
up, and he spent eighteen thousand years working like a
sonofabitch, and he got the heaven and earth parts sorted out
and stuck together.

"Then he died, so that all his work could live. His head

became the mountains, his breath the wind and the clouds, his voice became the thunder, his arms and legs became the four quarters of the earth, his blood the rivers and seas, his flesh the soil, his beard became the constellations in the sky, his skin and hair became the herbs and trees, his teeth and bones became the rocks and precious stones, his sweat became the rain.

"And the verminous insects creeping and crawling over his body, they became human beings."

We sit in silence. The mist is thicker now—like floating white rain. The ferryman speaks again in the same monotone. "Didn't even get a chuckle out of you—O.K., you don't gotta laugh. You paid your fare. That tiny light ahead, just over the water—that's where I'm taking you."

The mist dissolves, and the tiny light ahead resolves itself into a kerosene lantern hung off the stern of a black Chinese junk. We approach it slowly, and I can see it has black sails as well, furled at the moment. Miyoko puts a small pair of opera glasses in my hand. I take a closer look.

In the center of the deck, a man squats on a mat, his black robe clasped with coral. His moustache is long in the oriental fashion of another century, his face thin, ascetic. Before him is a low black lacquer table, on which is a lit alcohol lamp and a book. The flame is blue. He is reading. In the stern, a crowd of five or six tough looking men are playing fan-tan, spitting betel juice over the side.

Sir Rodney takes the glasses from my hand, looks through them a moment as we approach. He hands them back to me.

"The ship is the Black Bastard. The man in the center of the deck is the object of our little nautical foray. Wu Fang.

Wu is a pirate...as the philosopher has advised his disciples to flee debasing toil."

"The philosopher?"

"What he's reading. Confucius."

"How can you possibly see, at this distance, and in this light, what he's reading?"

Sir Rodney hesitates a moment before he answers me. "I don't see, Mr. Faber. I know Wu Fang. Very regular habits. He only has one book. He reads it. He practices piracy on a small scale. And he attends his temple."

I'm curious. "What temple?" I ask Sir Rodney.

"It's called, oddly enough, the Temple of Luck and Virtue."

The ferry bumps up against the side of the junk. We climb aboard. No one greets us or even notices our arrival. Sir Rodney is not surprised. He takes a seat on deck, across the mat from Wu Fang. Miyoko and I sit behind him. Silence, except for the murmur of the men in the stern, talking in low voices. Wu sits cross-legged, motionless, his eyes now shut, a silver pipe slanting down through slender fingers. The book of the philosopher lies open at his side. I can read the words at the top of the page, upside down, from where I'm sitting.

"Things have roots and branches. To know what precedes and what follows is nearly as good as having a head and feet."

The moon is at crescent. Wu nods slightly over the alcohol lamp in front of him, blue shadows flitting across his face. The pungent smell of opium is everywhere. The ash in

Wu's pipe still smoulders. It's hard to tell if he's alive or
dead. His pale green eyes are slits, and he dreams.

A dull warm wind slaps at the deck of the Black Bastard.
Sir Rodney is alert, twitching. Miyoko and I sit still behind
him. At last, Wu breaks the silence. He clacks an ivory fan.
His voice is smooth, sibilant.

"Sir Rodney. The pleasure given this worthless being by
the presence of yourself and your companions on the deck of
this miserable scrap of floating dung that fate and circum-
stance force me to call home is supreme, tainted only by the
pain felt in being unable to offer the comforts to which you
are accustomed."

Sir Rodney, nervous, body rocking, moustache quivering,
starts to respond, but Wu Fang raises one delicate hand.
Silence. Sir Rodney glances down at the black lacquer table,
sees his own reflection dimly, white moustache floating a
few feet below the dark surface. Wu speaks again, slowly,
evenly.

"Pray, be calm, Sir Rodney. Let's deal. Tell me what you
want." Sir Rodney turns his head back to me, whispers.

"One thing about dealing with Wu. He doesn't mind
long pauses in the conversation."

Sir Rodney is mentally preparing his pitch, and I'm
staring at the pirate's silver fingerguards, each of them
protecting a nail five inches long. Every one of the ten
guards depicts a scene from the hunt. On the middle finger,
left hand, the silver is worked into the image of a wild boar,
with his tusks imbedded in the thigh of the huntress, who
has her spear as firmly in the boar's back. Both of them are
calm, despite their pain and the contortion of their bodies.
The silver foliage around the rim might lead you to believe
the action takes place in a cultivated arbor rather than in the

wilderness. In the background a loving couple sits on a hilltop, arms entwined about each other, gazing at the scene below. My eyes refocus. Miyoko is still silent, but Sir Rodney is talking, more calmly now.

"My dear Wu Fang. It has come to my attention that you may be in possession of a rather large quantity of the keph. I have recently become interested in the purchase of such an item...."

Before Sir Rodney has finished speaking, a shoebox, wrapped in newspaper and tied with string, is deposited on the black lacquer table. Wu nods, waves his silver fingers over the box.

"Some weeks ago, my foolish and poorly disciplined crew mistakenly intercepted a small boat leaving Dr. Leroy's leprosarium dock, heading out across the bay. They were punished severely for this degrading transgression, which reflected poorly on the moral quality of the training to which I subject them. However, under the rear seat of the boat, as they were scavenging for food, they discovered this shoebox. It contains, my dear Sir Rodney, the largest single quantity of the keph drug I have ever seen. The violent imbeciles killed the boatman. The guilt I feel over this brutal savagery poisons my life.

"The keph is in the dried form, a pale crimson dust. This drug, Sir Rodney, is bad luck for me. I spend my life on the water, and do not wish to anger the dolphins. I'll let it go...cheap."

The deal is made. The ferry floats us back to New Jerusalem on a bay calm as black glass. Before we reach the pier, Sir Rodney gives me his final instructions.

"Meet us at Cowboy Dreamland in Change Alley tomor-

row night. Runme Singh will be there to pick up the package. You'll give your report that all went well. Later,
we meet at my motel. You'll find I am a generous
employer...."

I figure Sir Rodney's planning to switch boxes and hand a
phony over to Runme, then, when Runme discovers the
fake, tell him that Wu, or Leroy, made the switch on
him...so Rodney's in the clear. Or he might just hand the
keph over to Runme, and get a cut for himself. He takes less
chances that way...if the keph is in that box at all....

For a moment my mind fills with shoeboxes, wrapped in
newspaper and tied with string, floating through the streets
of New Jerusalem, waist high, slightly ruffling the air in
their wakes, nosing around corners, looking for a place to
set themselves down.

Sir Rodney lies back on the rough planking of the ferry,
his head in Miyoko's lap, box under his hand, eye on the
stars. I sit alongside him in silence, nothing in my heart or
head, mind out over the water.

CHANGE ALLEY

Strange events permit themselves the luxury of occurring. —Charlie Chan

I walk out through the empty lobby of the Cockpit Hotel. Windows broken, glass and garbage on the floor. The bar has been stripped clean. My gun is banging against my hip through my coat pocket. I'm feeling like a fool with the damn thing, but I'm ready, like the boy scouts.

I step outside the hotel entrance, and it's night. Only then I realize I must have slept all day. I unfold my map of the city, look for Change Alley where I'm to meet Sir Rodney and Runme Singh. I finally spot it, a dead end street off the lower end of Upper Phoenix Road.

I start walking, and there's something new in the night sky. Giant letters set out in a curving arc, N E W   J E R U-S A L E M in neon, shining out over the city, washing the rooftops in the green glow. Must be an old sign from the tourist days, and somebody's flipped it on for a little nos-

talgia. It's enormous, and parts of some of the letters are
missing.

My route to Upper Phoenix Road runs through crooked
and crowded alleys, smell of fish and rotted vegetables,
growing landscape of mold. Then I hit Arnheim Boulevard,
head north along it, a broad old-fashioned avenue lined with
trees. For a mile I don't see another human being. Nothing
moves but me.

A round-shouldered Chinese, one of the few who wear
traditional dress, the pigtail, black cotton robe, appears, a
tiny figure in the distance. He's shuffling south, toward me,
on the other side of Arnheim Boulevard—late for his all
night fan-tan game down by the docks, or hurrying home to
bed.

Picture this. Violet streetlamps hang over the empty
boulevard. On the east side is a man named Faber, reporter
from America. There I go. We approach each other on
opposite sides of the boulevard. Me and the Chinese are fifty
yards apart now—thirty—ten. When he's directly across
from me, the Chinese stops to light a long brown cigarette.
The flare of orange light across the broad avenue catches my
eye, and then it's gone. The Chinese keeps walking, moves
on until I can barely see him, a darker patch against the dark
at the far end of the boulevard.

Walking, and again there's Margo, back in my head, the
feelings still a jumble of anger and desire.

And then my mind jumps to a statement of Arnheim's,
printed as a preface in one of those tourist magazines. I
quote.

"This entire city was created so as to cast a shadow different from itself. This city is a device. While you visit New Jerusalem, I want you to think of yourselves moving through a miniature version of something a lot larger—in scope. Do you understand me?"

A small group of shops up ahead, and as I come closer, their lights go out one by one, doors closing. The face of the last shopkeeper disappears behind a green shutter. I'm feeling suddenly very lost, weak, and alone. I'm looking for something, I want something, and a shopkeeper's voice echoes in my head. . . .

". . . all sold out, Mister Man. We don't get no call for that sort of thing." Then behind my ear my mother and father whisper together, old voices in a sweet harmony. They're saying it's all right, but I know they are bloody comforters. They just been in the bathroom and wiped it clean and thrown the bloody paper in the bowl and flushed and got in there with their hands so I wouldn't see no red streaks when I went to piss, and they're telling me how it's OK, and it's too bad, and it don't matter that whatever I'm trying to find is gone. They're gonna help me look for it.

"Maybe it ain't dead, honey. Maybe it just got lost."

Forget them, Faber. Now that you're a big boy, you can travel: New Jerusalem, for example, where the birds cover the churchyard with an even layer of white as lime birdshit for Easter Sunday and it smells like autumn violets. The statues sing on their pedestals in the squares of the city, and the sun has a special whiteness it lends to everything. Bring the family, if you got one. We'll all dance together among the rat-faced citizens of New Jerusalem, the land that time forgot, the land that thieves and killers built, the land of truth, where it just lies on the highway like a dead dog and you can pick it up and write it down. Sure. I came here to tell it straight, and it gets more twisted all the time.

Change Alley. Tealeaf parlors, opium dens, live duck markets, tabernacles, flower girls, business academies, dental laboratories, office buildings full of cut-rate accountants, tuna with mayo on the client's phony receipts....

Cowboy Dreamland is at the alley's dead end—a low doorway with the skull of a Texas longhorn mounted above it. I reach out to knock, and a man with a hat closes his fingers around my wrist. "Doesn't open till after midnight, friend."

My meet with Sir Rodney can't happen till the joint opens. Time to kill. I move back down Change Alley, stand in a doorway, and I realize I'm searching for Margo in the crowd. My fury over what she did to me fades...I can even flatter myself by realizing that anyone else in New Jerusalem would've killed me for that box.

I try to think what it would be like to be born and raised here...and I picture me and Margo as the fox and the poisonous snake in the fable. They make a truce, and once they've agreed to be loving friends and partners, the snake bites. The fox is dying, and the snake calls him a fool. "You knew I was a snake...."

I fit. With Margo, it's harder to read the mix of what she does and what she is and what she might become.

I light a cigarette in the doorway. Pink neon ripples through Change Alley, then blue. Glint of an aluminum crutch. Violet streetlamp lights the bent back of the noodle-man, as he leans over his kettle in the dark, peering into the steam. Zuzu the pygmy stumbles by my doorway, baby carriage in front of her, looking for drunks to roll. Her leather face is a blur in the darkness. Shining silver tooth.

Seedy storefront down Change Alley, childish painting of a green rock on the door. I recognize the place—remember a blurry photo of the same door in *New Jerusalem, A Paradise For You*. It's the studio of the master of the Rock Bottom style of self-defense, based on the movements of large rocks as they roll on the bottom of the sea, stirred by the currents of the deep. The photo's caption claimed he was unconquerable, his spirit fine as dust, his body always moving with the waves.

But the story in New Jerusalem is that the master's skill is fading, and he's taken to pimping for a living. I've heard that students figure he's flipped. Every class in which he once insisted on strict discipline, respect for the art, and a perfection of body and spirit, is now relaxed and sloppy. He will often leave off teaching in the middle because one of his girls comes staggering in, drunk or bleeding. He has put the studio up for sale, but it's a little late to find a buyer in New Jerusalem.

The door on which the green rock is painted flies open. A young man with a crewcut steps out into Change Alley, closes the door behind him. My notebook's ready, and I ask some questions. He's Jason LeMay, a devoted student of the master's. After the master was dropped here for killing seven members of a New York street gang who tried to mug him, LeMay deliberately got himself sentenced to New Jerusalem to follow him. However, he's philosophical about it all.

"Well, I guess the old fart just couldn't keep it up anymore. Every once in a while he says, 'Why bother teaching these young people? They just use the art to feel important and pass the time. Better earn an honest dollar out of men's desire, and throw my own into the pot along with the rest.'"

LeMay gestures toward the door. "He's drinking more than ever, the walls of the academy are covered with crude drawings of sex organs, and the students have ceased being westerners, who were the bulk of the pupils before the change. Now there's only old Chinese men, sit around drink tea, gossiping, occasionally get up to do a bit of the Rock Bottom form."

I learn that these events have inspired the master of the rival academy. LeMay points to a wooden door I had not noticed before exactly across the narrow lane. It's covered with a painting of a porcupine, rampant.

"He's the Master of the Hedgehog style, which involves the wearing of suits of leather armor covered over in sharp steel spines. The armor is complete with gloves and face-mask, cunningly designed so you can throw the quills off any portion at the opponent. This rival challenged the Master of the Rock Bottom style to single combat to the death. You know what the master said?"

"I'll bite," I tell him, "what'd he say?"

"If he wants to fool around, I'll fool around...."

At the corner of Change Alley and Arnheim Quay is the New Jerusalem Museum, a converted Arab nightclub that used to be called Sheba's Breasts. Two dome construction. Fading poster of a belly-dancer under cracked glass. I stopped in there the other day, on my way to the harbor.

The museum has two categories of exhibits. In the East Breast: memorabilia and documents relating to the life of Arnheim, including pieces of his clothing, his one published book (translation of the Sea Dyak bible), a lock of his hair under glass, architectural drawings for certain major constructions in New Jerusalem, out-of-focus photographs of the great man, features indistinct. A recent addition to this collection are large wall posters of poems about Arnheim's greatness, written by Runme Singh.

The West Breast contains artifacts of the world from which the citizens of New Jerusalem are excluded. These of necessity are very old, and the fruit of smuggling: a rusted toaster sits atop a marble pedestal; faded editions of *Time, Motor Trend, Consumer Reports;* an antique HomEnt Unit with a five foot screen; a Mr. Coffee machine, exhibited upside down; sections of indecipherable machinery; transistor boards.

I bang on the front door of the museum with my fist. It's late, but if there's a caretaker, I figure he might let a reporter in. I've still got time until Cowboy Dreamland opens. After the human carousel of Change Alley, a little quiet would settle my head.

No one answers. I walk around toward a door on the side of the East dome. On it is a rusted brass plate: "Quang T. Lee, Assistant Curator." No answer to my knock. Light at a window. I peep through, down into a room full of mops, large drums of cleaning fluid. A man in his underwear, who I assume is Quang T. Lee, sits on a chair under a swaying light bulb, studying a copy of the magazine *Loving Couples*. He stares at one photo in particular. It's a moment before I realize he's masturbating. The photo he is looking at is in black and white, and printed badly. It shows a young man lying face down on a bed, his ass stuck up, and astride him, facing the reader, is a woman, also naked, except for black sunglasses. She looks like Miyoko Yakimoto. There is a balloon coming out of her mouth. It reads: "Go horsie! Go horsie!" In her right hand is a ping-pong paddle.

Across the small room is an old display case. A sign on the case reads "Model of a Section of the Diorama: SOUTH-DURING THE MONSOON," and in smaller letters, "De-stroyed by vandals in the chaos after Arnheim's death." Under the dusty glass, what appears to be a model of part of the city of New Jerusalem. In the tiny streets, little figures running, arms above their heads to shield themselves from a storm. One figure pushes a baby carriage.

Quang's thin thighs are flapping in and out now, and though I hate to interrupt a man at his pleasures, I knock again, this time louder. I can hear the shuffling of his worn carpet slippers on the rush matting of the floor. Then his voice whispers through the immovable door.

"All closed now. All dark inside. Whoever you are, go home to bed." The thin line of yellow light under the door goes out.

Farther down Change Alley, I glance at a low office building. The building has a neon sign that reads: "IN-

VESTMENT OPPORTUNITIES" in blinking pink. I read the signs on the office windows on the second floor: Blanco and Sal Tartaragus Resorts Development Company; Sadharma Pundarika Orphans Relief Fund; Puckle's Machinery Company; Holy Island Salt Works; Animal Hair Trading Corporation; Acme Mirror Works; Perpetual Motion League; Wo Hong Fan-Tan Society.

Late night open air betting parlours, where wagers are taken on every conceivable chance. One sleepy looking man places a bet on the date of his own death. Long odds. I figure I've got a way to get down on a good thing, but the bookies have stopped taking any action on the arrival time or purpose of the ship. Odds on the subject fluctuated too violently, and the bettors were going in way over their heads. Too bad. I could make a killing. The Kamoro cult has it wrong, and they're as certain as Runme Singh that they've got it right.

Your everyday inhabitant of the penal colony of New Jerusalem, however, doesn't have it either way. If you asked him, he'd tell you nothing's gonna happen. Runme Singh made the official government announcement of the island's closing down, and some people believed it, but for a hell of a lot of them it's a case of the boy who's cried wolf. Runme's told a few whoppers to the populace, and now some of them won't believe this one—especially because the boy ain't crying wolf. He's crying your whole world's gonna end and a man's gonna come and take you to another one. Who's gonna believe that? It's just as reasonable to think that this great white ship full of automatic dishwashers and mobile homes is gonna show up and cover the island with gravy.

In the bend of Change Alley a small park, where, under a pergola, the New Jerusalem orchestra is tuning up for its evening dansant...a motley collection of gamelans, tubas, a piccolo, shaku-hachi, and kettledrums. The conductor is a local character who's been pointed out to me: Sergei Kovonovsky, a disaffected artiste sent to New Jerusalem by mother Russia. They warm up, and swing into the obbligato. Sergei is passionate, and it shows. He can snuffle up strong tea with butter through his beard with the best of them. The edges of his red silk tie are frayed. "Bravo! Bravo!"

The story here is that Sergei believes New Jerusalem is God's demented fancy, conceived to torment him alone. Nothing has come of his stay here but suffering and unsatisfied desire, which he has learned to transform directly into music. "Bravo! Bravo!"

I stroll behind the bandstand, glow of Change Alley at my back, down a path into a wooded area of the park. Quieter here, and I'm trying to think it all over, head full of too many impressions, and my impressions of the impressions. The trees very quickly get thick; a wall of branches bars my way. I sit down in the dark under a tree, the orchestra playing a samba in the distance. I feel cut off from this world for a moment, hid by the night and the trees....

Arnheim was as varied with his plantings as he was with his architecture, though with the vegetation, his work can be seen in its original form. Nobody's fucked with it. The trees of New Jerusalem are the banyan, oak, sandalwood, maple, bho, spanish chestnut, black locust, hickory, elm, cinnamon, and baobab.

The people of New Jerusalem have unsuccessfully adapted to twenty-first century life. And why? Cause they're not living it. They got an excuse. Add it up: the citizens of New Jerusalem are not detached, narcissistic, or randomly violent. They are attached, vain, and violent for various reasons, good or no. They are greedy, lustful, and occasionally repentant. Work is real to almost all of them. Family is real to most of them. So are sex and shame. In this place, all the nerves are bare. There are people here who can steal, scheme, or chant wildly in the blinding sun—then, at home, when rain comes, these same people sit quietly under their eaves. Many houses are equipped with translucent rain gutters, in which the water sparkles. One of the chief pleasures of these people is to gaze for hours at these hypnotic motions of light, trapped in the water.

Back to Change Alley. Cowboy Dreamland has its door open, loud American country music pouring out into the street. I'm walking toward the place, when a ragged peasant scuttles past me into a sidestreet like a crab, a silver coin flashing from between his lips. He's gone. A hand reaches slowly out from a second story window, embroidered sleeve, red dragons far away over Mount Arnheim, first lightning before the rains. . . .

I'm standing at the door, longhorn skull above me, a tug at my pants leg. The shoe shine boy from outside the hotel is there, with his tray of junk for sale. He sings his little song.
    "Shoelace, chiclet, Green Spot, 'larm clock. . ." He hands me a telegram. "For you, Mister Man." It's dated some days before, and is from my editor.

"FABER. AM HOLDING SIX COLUMNS FRONT PAGE
YOUR STORY. IT BETTER BE GOOD. REMEMBER. AS
FAR AS MY READERS ARE CONCERNED NEW JERU-
SALEM NOT THERE. WHAT IS THERE IS YOUR
STORY."

His readers. . . the bastard. I crumple up the telegram, toss
it into the street. I go inside.

AT COWBOY DREAMLAND, AND AFTER

> *This atmosphere...is not made of air at all,*
> *but of ghost—the substance of souls blended*
> *into one immense translucency, souls of people*
> *who thought in ways never resembling our*
> *ways. Whatever mortal man inhales that*
> *atmosphere, he takes into his blood the thrilling*
> *of these spirits; and they change the sense*
> *within him.*
>
> —Lafcadio Hearn, *Kwaidan*

The front door to Cowboy Dreamland leads to an open
courtyard with a dirt floor, and I'm there a moment before I
realize that I am on set: a barrel cactus, dusty Ford pickup
with a paper mâché driver, gun rack at the back of the cab
holds a Winchester 30-30. On the other side of the courtyard
a wax statue of an Indian brave squats by a campfire. Sound
track of coyotes, owl hoots, Union Pacific long ago and far
away. They sure know how to make an American boy feel at

141

home. I cross the courtyard, enter through two swinging
doors marked BAR AND GRILL.

The dance floor is full. The house band at Cowboy
Dreamland is the Mandarins: Matthew Tan on vocals and
saxophone, Chopstick Charlie on drums, Nathan Watanabe
on pedal steel (number one on the Japanese charts till a child
molesting charge sent him down through the clouds to New
Jerusalem), Freezing Point Nelson on bass.

The band cultivates an absolute absence of contact with its
audience while onstage. They stare into space, motionless as
possible. The technique is to focus on the keph (when they
got it), beating in the river of blood in a narrow vein in their
foreheads. They are the best four man band I've ever heard
in my life. Between sets, however, they are vulgar and
obnoxious, pawing the customers, making obscene sug-
gestions, farting into the faces of people over their dinners.

The Mandarins are costumed as depraved orientals of the
aristocracy, court of the Dowager Empress, before the Boxer
Rebellion. Floor length embroidered robes, chin whiskers.
Once a night they put on cowboy hats in deference to the
management. Matthew Tan has a fake Fu Manchu moustache that is waxed and perfumed, falls to his waist. His
instrument is a Bo Diddley special made long ago in Hong
Kong, a square of red plastic with the word SILENCE
spelled out along the neck in mother-of-pearl.

I take a table in a far corner. A waitress dressed like a
dimestore Dale Evans shows up. I check the menu.

"Gimme the blue-plate special and a Green Spot."

Then I glimpse her through the dancers, on the other side
of the crowded club. It's Margo, sitting alone at a small

round table. For a moment, she's obscured by shuffling couples; then I see her again. She lights a cigarette, looks down into her drink to see how the ice cube is doing. Waiting. I check the urge to run across the dance floor, grab my chair and keep myself in it. Better not make any moves till the rest of the players arrive.

I check out the clientele. All the usual New Jerusalem elite and riff-raff. I spot Sir Rodney and Miyoko, up and dancing. Miyoko carries a large shoulder bag, with a curiously shoebox-shaped bulge in it—either the keph or some red dust a chemist made up in a back alley that morning—a little powdered milk, a little quinine, a little red food coloring.

Matthew Tan and the Mandarins are playing one of their own compositions, the up-tempo number "Nothing Ever Dies." Miyoko minces gracefully to the music. Sir Rodney's dancing style is cramped by his constantly looking over his shoulder as if he expected someone to knife him in the back. He finally spots me as the music ends. As he and Miyoko bow to each other, Sir Rodney gives me a sly wink. He's worried I'll forget my lines. I wink back, and see that the waitress, coming my way, caught the exchange. Her expression tells me she's sure I'm a lunatic, and I find I couldn't care less. I don't know how many games she's playing, but I know how many some of the players are playing, and the levels of sincerity and/or deception involved make insanity a moot point. If anyone isn't exactly on your level, at a given moment, they're quite likely to think you're insane.

She sets the Blue Plate Special down—American cuisine. It's meat loaf and mashed, and the cook in this place is a genius. His gravy dipper hit the exact center of the ice-cream scoop of mashed potatoes, and the puddle of hot country gravy sits there in its white shell like a perfect little lake filling the crater of Mount Arnheim.

I look around for the kitchen, spot a square opening in the back wall with a screen door on it. The screen buzzes with flies. The cook opens the door suddenly and the flies take off. He drops a bowl of chili on the pick-up ledge. He's a round-shouldered Chinese with a pigtail, looks expressionlessly at the dancers. I remember him from somewhere... man I saw once across an empty boulevard, orange glow from his cigarette. Someone yells "Fry two"; the screen door slams shut and the cook disappears.

I don't have long to wait for the main event. Through the doors staggers Runme Singh himself, badly disguised as a drunken sailor. He wears a dirty white sailor suit, dark glasses. The band is playing, and Runme bangs across the dance floor, bumping into everyone, singing choruses of "Heave away, Johnny Boy" at the top of his lungs.

One woman is staring suspiciously at him. The drunken sailor leers back, points between his legs. He shouts into her face.

"I gotta snake tattoo runs right around my dick inna spiral. Wanna see it?" He figures he's vulgar enough to keep even this clientele at a distance, and he's right.

He's making his sloppy way over to Margo's table. Runme's got a few yards to go, and I let my eyes leave him, travel around the room, past the moose antlers, a stuffed puma, war bonnet made in Taiwan. I spot one of Runme's guards near the door, eye on his boss. His machine gun is camouflaged as an umbrella.

Then I notice a big man at a table by himself. He's motionless, a row of empty beers in front of him. His eyes are also fixed on Runme. Those eyes are very blue—Harry the Horse. He wears a frayed dark suit, a bowtie, his blond hair slicked back on his head. His feet are propped up on the table and if his eyes weren't wide open and moving he'd seem asleep in the din.

A look at Harry and you can tell his brain is diffuse—in the blood. He's simply let it wither on its bony stem. Harry does his thinking with his spinal cord, in the body, through and through him.

Runme and Margo whisper intently to each other for a few minutes, as the Mandarins tune up their instruments. The band breaks into a fierce rhumba, and Sir Rodney and Miyoko return to the dance floor. Runme spots Miyoko's shoulder bag, and with a grin of triumph he can't suppress, he rhumbas out toward them.

Margo's eyes follow the back of Runme's sailor suit through the weaving bodies. We've got separate seats but we're watching the same show. Matthew Tan tickles the microphone with his tongue.

"I started out to go to Coooba, ended up at Miami Beach. It's not so very far from Coooba, and oh what a Rhumba they teach!"

Runme, Miyoko, and Sir Rodney are dancing together now, a funloving threesome. Miyoko wriggles a shoebox, wrapped in newspaper and tied with string, out of her bag.

Runme slips it under his coat, rhumbas in my direction. Sir
Rodney gives me a tremendous wink behind Runme's
retreating back. Miyoko and Sir Rodney dance off toward
their table, as Runme plops drunkenly into the empty chair
across from me. He is cold sober.

"Well?" he says, "did you see the transaction?"

I tell him the details of Sir Rodney's meeting with Wu
Fang, managing to forget the little chitchat between Sir
Rodney, Miyoko, and myself. As I talk, Runme Singh
keeps rubbing the shoebox with his palms. He loves it, he
does.

I finish my speech, and Runme looks satisfied. He lays his
hand on my shoulder.

"I won't forget your services, Mr. Faber. I remember that
little newspaper you're planning to buy. Your interview
with me might give it the send-off it needs."

Runme pauses a moment to get his act back together. He
overdoes it, falling clumsily out of his chair, knocking my
plate onto the floor. When he gets up his sailor suit is
smeared with gravy. He doesn't notice. He leans toward me,
whispers, "Kamoros everywhere! Tomorrow night is New
Jerusalem's last night of existence. Special performance in
the National Theatre. Be there. Meet me in my box."

Runme rolls his eyes, falls backwards, again crashing to
the floor in feigned drunkenness. He staggers up, the box
under his coat, heads for the door. "Heave awaaaaay,
Johnny Boy...Heave awaaaaay!" His bodyguard follows
him out.

Harry the Horse rises from his table like a blond bronto-
saurus lifting himself out of a long swamp sleep. He blinks,

and follows Runme, at a respectable distance, out Cowboy Dreamland's front door. If I worried about Runme's health, I'd be glad he had a bodyguard with him, and probably a few more outside. I imagine Harry is aware of Runme's company. He looks like he's in no hurry at all.

Sir Rodney and Miyoko dance toward the door. They stop at my table, Sir Rodney checking in to see if I've done my duty. I tell him I gave him straight A's in sportsmanship and a good conduct medal besides—and Runme bought it. Sir Rodney is properly grateful.

"Meet us at the motel tomorrow afternoon, Faber. You can join us at the opening of the Pyramid of Cheops, the opening of the Virgin Gate, the opening of the Third Eye— the opening, Faber, of the box!"

"What motel are you at?"

This question puzzles Sir Rodney, but fortunately, Miyoko looks up the answer in a small black notebook.

"The Blue Spruce," she says.

"I got it. I'll be there."

"That, Mr. Faber, is excellent," says Sir Rodney. He wraps one long arm around Miyoko's tiny waist, and they bump out the doors, leave them swinging back and forth behind them.

I get up, make my way over to Margo's table. I don't know how long she's been watching me, but my appearance is no news. She looks up at me through the smoke.

"Faber, sit down. You've had too much to drink." I try to remember the cold stone of the Bridge of Monkeys against my face, try to hate the little bitch...No good. She's too beautiful, and besides, I look into her face and I can see that she's forgotten it. In Margo's head, that part's over.

I sit down, and I'm feeling good just looking at her...one of those moments when you know a woman might look ordinary to anyone else, but you can see her beauty, and it runs very deep.

I figure to let her begin. She's seen me with Rumme and Sir Rodney, and she has to be curious. She just fingers her black cashmere sweater. She doesn't say a word, just looks right back at me. We're not gonna be talking if I don't start. I do.

"What'd he tell you?"

"Who?" she says, and looks over my shoulder at the dance floor. She's worried about something. I can see myself backlit in her pupils, little Faber twins looking quite mysterious in those tiny prisons.

"Daddy."

She takes her time before she answers.

"He's not my Daddy, and I think he sent me out to get hurt. He knew Kamoros would be watching me. Bait for Big Tiny, to distract him. I think he guessed Leroy's package might be a phony...."

I sit there, trying to take it in. I ask the obvious. "That was your fake Big Tiny tossed into Mount Arnheim yesterday?"

"Yeah," says the lady. "I made it up to give Runme. Then two of those bastards stole it from me on the Bridge of Sand."

"Then you've still got Leroy's package. Don't you know what's in it?"

"It looks right, but I didn't try it yet." Margo stands up.

"Come on, Faber. Come home with me. I promise you, this time you'll wake up where you lie down. We'll play who's got the button." She looks me in the eye. "It better be me."

As I follow her across the dance floor toward the door, the Mandarins hit a few strong minor chords, begin to sing in a kind of gospel harmony. Margo stops to listen.

Everybody's sleeping—at the Zombie Jamboreeeeee,
Everybody's singing—at the Zombie Jamboreeeeee,
Everybody's dancing—at the Zombie Jamboreeeeee....

Margo needs to yell over the music: "My favorite. Too bad we'll miss the last dance." She moves toward the door as Matthew Tan's voice breaks into falsetto and the guitars screech feedback till the ceiling shakes....

"Everybody's laughing—at the Zombie Jamboreee,
Zombie Jamboreeee!"

The doors swing shut behind us, and we're in the New Jerusalem night. Margo's step is quick and light as a child's. Me, Faber, your reporter—I keep up with her, one foot after the other.

Margo and I in her apartment, lights of the harbor below. I sit down on a low couch. I'm impatient.

"Well, bring it out."

Margo looks at me in a funny way. "You *are* from outside, aren't you?"

I ask her what she means.

"You don't treat keph that way."

"What if it ain't the keph?" I tell her.

"What if it is," she says, and I can see she's hoping a lot harder than she'd like....

Margo goes into the bathroom. She's taking a long, slow

bath. I wait. She comes out a half-hour later, wrapped in an enormous red beach towel, her black hair tangling wet around her face, down onto the white of her shoulders. My favorite colors.

She doesn't even know I'm there. She lights a candle. She places the shoebox we stole from Dr. Leroy on the coffee table. She kneels, opens it. Red dust. She slides a finger across her lips, licks it with her tongue. She dips her finger into the dust. She loosens the towel around her, and lets it fall to the floor. She stands, slowly rubs the drug into the inside of her thigh.

She stares into her mirror, waiting for her body to glow, waiting for the panther tattooed on her belly to writhe up and chew on her nipple, waiting for the world to sink into the sea.

Her mouth opens slightly, and her voice is small. "Nothing. Nothing from outside, nothing from inside." Margo's face changes, becomes darker, more flushed with blood. She murmurs to herself, and I catch some of the words. She's trying to wish her mother up from hell, where she had consigned her a few weeks ago. Without the keph it is impossible.

Margo's eyes glaze over in fury. Her naked body shakes, and to stop the shaking she digs her nails into the inside of her thigh. Five even streaks of blood. She turns her back to me, walks to her window, looks out over New Jerusalem. When she turns to me again, the pain has left her face. She pulls on a Chinese robe, produces a plastic garbage bag, dumps the red dust into it, along with the shoebox.

"Nada," she says. "Red milk sugar. We don't got it and that has got to change. I am not sailing on any fucking rehab boat to get off and wash dishes in Uncle John's all night cafe, end up whoring on the outside for a pimp like you, Faber. Not this little girl. We're getting it...but not tonight. I'm exhausted."

Margo finds a flat leather case, takes out a silver hypodermic needle, goes to the refrigerator, and takes out a small ampoule of clear liquid. Needle bounces through red rubber seal. Margo draws back the plunger till the ampoule is drained. She looks over at me.

"It's just sleepytime stuff. No dreams tonight...." The needle slides in smooth like the skin wasn't there. Margo lies back on the couch. "You don't feel anything," she says, "but a coldness under the skin." Some kind of sweet narcotic. Her head falls softly to one side, opening the strong lines of her neck. She whispers now, and I have to kneel down to hear her.

"Faber, I'm scared. I'm scared to leave New Jerusalem. What's out there?" I don't want to tell her, and I start to try anyway, till I see she's sleeping. The Chinese robe is tangled around her naked body like a baby's blanket...red sash, dragons over mountains. I sit down on the floor next to her and stroke her hair. Her back. She purrs in her sleep.

Now close eyes little baby and take your rest. I'm thinking of you. In the meadow a black pony dances. See you bye and bye. Sweet dreams, Margo, and nighty-night.

I stand up, stretch, look at her lying there. I'm awake, feeling lively and a little wired. Four A.M. Time to give you the news.

BULLETIN: Dateline, New Jerusalem—Forces beyond our control are operating and we are about to capsize. We are gonna flip, end up upside down—that is, if we started upright. I can feel the beginning of that last rollover in my head, and it's making me nervous, believe me.

Or somebody is about to split this world like splitting a fish for the frypan, up the belly and we're all falling out into the sky curled up in little balls, seeds on the wind. Everyone aboard is presumed lost. Ain't it the truth.

Find them. That's the job. Find them and help them and help yourself. Give 'em a five dollar bill and a loaf of bread and tell 'em Christ Jesus is waiting—in the next town down the road, by the railroad station under the catalpa trees by the wayside he's waiting, and to pass the time he's in a card game with some railroad men under the trees. If they hurry they can catch him before he heads north to check his traplines—beaver, otter, some red squirrel. Richest country I've ever seen and no lie. Paradise.

I lie down alongside Margo, and I'm still talking; the rest is a whisper into her hair. . . . You come up there with me, girl, and we'll be living on chicken and wine. All our days will be fat as melons, and when the sun shines we'll take it personal.

KAMORO FOLLIES

For the pre-logical mind, everything is a
miracle, or rather, nothing is; and therefore,
everything is credible, and there is nothing
either impossible or absurd. —L. Levy-Bruhl,
How Natives Think,
trans. L.A. Clare

Morning. Margo leads me out to the nearest stop on the local version of mass transit, the New Jerusalem Railroad. A simple low building, painted pink with a pagoda top, sits by the tracks. A large sign over the entrance reads: "RIGHT EYEHOLE," and is accompanied by an equally large styled drawing of a human eye.

I ask about it, notebook in hand, reporter face on, and I get another one of those looks that tells me Margo thinks I'm putting her on. No one could be that stupid.

"It's the name of the stop," she tells me.

"Why?" is my next question. With that she decides I'm hopeless, and leaves me standing there while she goes to the

153

ticket window. I half expect the railroad to be closed down, the workers having got the news. Nope. Business as usual. Either they've heard the ship is coming and they don't believe it, or they haven't heard, or they're dedicated public servants gonna hang in there till the choo-choo makes its final run.

I'm about to ask to find out which, when the train pulls in. It's a small steam locomotive with two bright blue and yellow passenger cars behind the tender. Cute. We get on board.

We are headed out to a crocodile farm the Kamoro cult maintains on the far side of the island of New Jerusalem. "Just raising crockodillos for the handbag trade, Officer," says Big Tiny. Hide farming is the front. The farm is actually the site of all major cult activities.

"Important show today," Margo tells me. She figures if Big Tiny has an angle on the keph, he might show his hand. The day's ceremony is called REVELATION OF THE GLOWING BEING OF THE KEPHI-BOY. Your reporter stops himself from asking her about that one, but Margo catches my curiosity anyway. She shrugs her shoulders.

"I've just heard the name of it...do you think those Kamoro bastards give me the agenda? We can get to view the ceremony, though—maybe take a look around." She's got an in everywhere.

Margo's guess is today's ritual is a sort of preface to the major celebration, WELCOME TO THE BOAT OF THE GODS, taking place at the harbor at dawn tomorrow.

"Airport control's been receiving the ship's signals. It's no secret. Today, and then one more night of New Jerusalem. Some people must be in a helluva hurry," Margo says, and I realize we're included.

We pull up at a stop called "RIGHT NOSEHOLE." When we pull away, I ask again about the railroad. Here's the story on that one.

The New Jerusalem Railroad runs around the island. There are twelve stops: RIGHT EYEHOLE (Heaven's Eye), LEFT EYEHOLE (Earth's Eye), RIGHT EARHOLE (God's Ear), LEFT EARHOLE (Satan's Ear), RIGHT NOSEHOLE (In-breath), LEFT NOSEHOLE (Outbreath), MOUTHHOLE (Eater-upper), PISSHOLE, SHITHOLE, BELLYHOLE (Navel), DEATHHOLE (Topknot), LIFEHOLE (Jade Gate, Square of Heaven Between the Eyes).

This transit system was designed by the renowned Professor Nakana, who is also the architect of Arnheim Bird Park, a landscaping fantasy based on an obscure volume of pornographic tales by the homeless monk Lu Chien, who also, due to his constant need for protection as a result of his abrasive personality, founded the Rock Bottom style of self-defense.

Professor Nakana based his transit design on the classics: The *Nei Pien* of Ko Hung, the *Manifestation of Change in the Mountains*, the *Flow and Return to Womb and Tomb*, and the eight trigrams of the *I-Ching*. The stops are the twelve breaks in the broken lines, so that all stopping places are yin. The track is yang.

When the limousine arrived to take Professor Nakana to the dedication ceremony, where he was to drive a golden spike to complete construction, Arnheim's chauffeur found his house empty. A charred copy of the I-Ching was in the center of the coffee table. Nakana himself was found three days later in the jungles outside New Jerusalem, wandering blindly among the vines, as he had lost his glasses.

He never again spoke a word. From that day twenty-five years ago to the present, he has attempted to communicate only in unintelligible signs. These signs seem to have reference to the concepts of motion and rest, and to the notion that his transit system is a blueprint, or signal, that may cause some actuality to come into being. This point in his gesturing is always followed by vomiting and convulsions.

Professor Nakana has been confined for a number of years. From his barred window in the Leprosarium and Clinic for Rare Diseases, he is able to see the central terminal, where the trains begin and end their run.

The Kamoro farm. "Margo! So glad! And Mr. Faber! Come right this way." The greeters are a phony British planter type with his East Indian boy, left over from when things needed to look good for the tourists. They stayed on. We're a big chance to run the old routine.

The pathway glitters in the sunlight, and crackles as I walk along it. The East Indian's turban bobs in front of Margo and me. He points underfoot.

"Champagne glasses, sah. Sahib tosses them out his library window in the evening, after toasting a birth among the gators. This year lots of little crockadillos, sah, lots of champagne glasses. Make the road go tingle-tingle."

The cult's main industry is this crocodile breeding, and they're stacking the hides in a vast godown by the docks, storing them up as a gift for when the gods arrive. They cart the gators, live, at night; icy water leaks a trail from the wagons into the midnight soil of New Jerusalem, heading down toward Harry the Horse's place by the docks. Black tin roof, stink of crocodiles, moonlight on the verandah. Harry sits waiting, lonesome toothpick in his teeth, knife already sharp. He skins them out, probably drinks the crocodile blood to make him strong. There they go, moonlight on the wet back of a crocodile, sunlight on the pathway of broken champagne glasses. . . .

An unctuous aide of Big Tiny's, Hawaiian shirt, his kamoro made of black vinyl stuffed with weeds, takes over.

"Here to view the boy, Mr. Faber? Publicity is hardly necessary in his case, but it was kind of you to come. Please join the other guests on the patio. Have a Green Spot while the devotees prepare themselves."

Lawn chairs, an iron flamingo. There are no other guests. Margo sits down, and takes out a small snakeskin bound notebook and an antique ballpoint pen. She takes notes in a small feminine hand. She is trying to dope out the location of the real box of keph, as if the whole thing was some sort of game of logic—or illogic.

She has the names of all the main figures in New Jerusalem affairs at the top: Runme Singh, herself, Big Tiny, Wu Fang, Dr. Leroy, Sir Rodney. My name is there as well, and I'm not sure why. Through Dr. Leroy's name she draws a thin X. Below are a group of rectangular boxes. Each box has a question mark in it, except one with an X drawn through it and a tiny volcano drawn below, and another with a darker X drawn through it. I figure that's the one she tried. There are others, and she's working on a drawing of one more, with a tiny kamoro below it.

I step up quietly behind her. She's deep in concentration, her tongue sticking out between her lips. I touch it with my finger, and it slides inside. I bury my other hand under dark hair, against the back of her neck. It is muscular, slightly damp. Margo does not move, pen poised over the paper.

At that moment, the East Indian arrives with mint juleps, and a long line of marchers begin their steady tramp out of the ritual barn into the clearing in front of us. Each man or woman is naked, except for the kamoros strapped across their faces. I spot a Canon, two old Minoltas, and a rusty Leica among the usual crowd of busted instamatics and homemade articles. These must be obduratos at the head of the class.

Their chant begins; names of the gods rise up in the clearing: "Sannnnyo! Magnavox! Motorola!" There's a fat man among the dancers, scraps of luggage tags decorating his arms and legs, wraparound sunglasses under his toothpaste box kamoro. It's Petersen, and I notice in his hand a scrap of red cellophane. Then I realize they all have them. Margo whispers to me.

"They'll slap them over their viewfinders in a minute. World turns to blood. The gods failed them when their prayer cycle was in Supplication at the volcano. Now the cycle is in Anger. They'll go a little nuts before the cycle returns to its first position, Silent Plea. They could do anything."

I whisper back to her little pink ear. "Let's get the hell out of here."

"No. We've got to see the Kephi-boy...and see if we can get hold of what they've been feeding him...."

"Maybe Tiny's got nothing," I answer. "If they were hot enough to rob you of what they thought was the real thing, maybe they've run out of the stuff...."

"Maybe," says Margo, "and maybe they found some more."

In a moment, at some signal everybody catches but me, all the cult members slap their red cellophane over their viewfinders. They begin a ferocious and awkward kind of dancing and jumping. Some of them slap themselves on their naked asses and thighs. A woman whirls by close to us, her fists clenched, beating at her breasts and ribs. Furious screaming of the names of the gods, till I'm holding my stomach on the ground laughing, and a little frightened, and then I'm just feeling crazy. Margo wonders what's so funny, and I think of explaining to her about the names, and then I say, "Nothing's funny," and I mean it.

A small raised platform made of logs is wheeled out into the clearing, and bonfires are lit in a circle around it. Big Tiny mounts the platform, and the crowd begins to quiet.

Petersen wanders out of the throng near us, sweat pouring down his pudgy body. He's been dancing up a storm. He's made holes in his credit cards, and they dangle off his penis, tied there with string. I'm staring and he laughs in my face.

"Getting all this, Faber? Where's your notebook? Write it down."

"Have fun, Petersen," is all I can think to say.

"You might be wondering why I don't let these people in on the origin of their deities, and what the ship is actually coming for. I prefer to let them have their moment in the sun. Their disappointment tomorrow morning is bound to be severe. That is the last advice I'm giving you, Faber. And there's a trailer to that story. Don't get in my way."

Margo turns her head, very slowly, away from the ceremony to look at him. She's been listening.

"Is this Margo?" says Petersen. He's about to say something else, but Margo has a big gob of spit rolled up on her tongue. Her lips part, and she flips the gob of spit onto Petersen's face.

He wipes it off with his palm. "Little bitch!" he screams, and he goes for her. I shove him back, one hand into his sweaty belly, backhand him hard across the face with the other. It knocks his kamoro loose, and it dangles by his ear.

No one notices us. Up on the makeshift podium someone hands Big Tiny a cardbard megaphone. Petersen is backing away.

"She's really hateful, Faber. She has no morals at all, you know. Gutter cunt." Petersen cools a bit or he's faking. He seems amused by us again.

"I hope you're planning on pimping for her when the ship gets back to America, Faber. If not, I'd let her go her own way. I doubt she has the keph, and she's very thin.

"You'll both excuse me. I've got to bring out the boy. He can't actually make it on his own, you see...."

Petersen is gone, and Big Tiny's voice booms out over the crowd. He's full of shit from the beginning, but they're taking it all in, and I can see why. Big Tiny is the best streetcorner preacher I've ever heard. He's passionate and he's brilliant, and if he's faking it and doesn't believe what he's saying, then he's also the best goddamn liar I've ever seen.

Tiny is selling them the idea that the ship is loaded with all the artifacts of what's known as modern life. The old ones remember, the memories twisted and blurred by years in New Jerusalem. The young ones, born here, can only fantasize, based on legends, fragments of Arnheim's architecture and smuggling, or pictures in faded magazines. They'll have it all, courtesy of the gods—and the tourists will return, and there will be tipping once again in the land.

Tiny is so good I have a hard time not jumping up and down and yelling "Glory! Glory!" He feeds it to them backwards, tells them the outside is coming inside, instead of the inside disappearing into the outside—and they eat it up.

And then Petersen is on the platform as well, and he is leading a child. He puts the boy's hand in Big Tiny's and gets off there. The crowd goes crazy. Margo is staring, her mouth open. I don't blame her. The kid is something to see.

The Kephi-boy is about five years old, and thin to the point of emaciation. He has a brand new Nikon camera strapped to his head, and the weight of it brings his neck forward in a permanent bend. He's had it there all his life. The camera's metal shines. The boy's skin is coffee-colored, but splotched with a bluish pink on his cheeks and right side. His nails and hair have never been cut. He wears a little robe of what looks like fish skin.

Big Tiny wraps his powerful hands around the boy's waist and holds him high in the air. Cheers and screams as his little face takes the sunlight. His eyes are all pupil, dead black. The rest of the boy's face looks as if it had no bones, just skin stuffed randomly with meat. One corner of his mouth flops open and he drools down his chin and onto his neck in a steady stream. Tiny sets him down. The boy collapses on the platform.

Someone throws a blanket over his body, and then Big Tiny takes a giant step. Now he's standing astride the kid like a colossus, and he starts talking, reeling off the Kephi-boy's history, his pedigree—that he's been fed the keph with his mother's milk and his creamed farina every day of his life on earth, that the dolphins worship him, that he is the reincarnation of the wisdom of Arnheim, that he *wills* the ship to come tomorrow and bring them all the goodies and tourists they pray for. And I know through all of it that this time, about the boy, Tiny is lying—and he knows it. He takes a deep breath and outs with the biggest promise of all. The boy, who has never spoken a word, is soon going to speak, and he knows the formula for making the keph as his bones know it, and he will teach it to the cult. Tiny is ranting now, almost out of control, and the crowd ain't much better.

"No longer will Runme Singh" (Boos, cries of "Kill!" from the mob) "rob us of our gifts! No more will they bribe the gods with keph! We alone will know it, and it will lead us to our kingdom!"

Margo is still staring at the crumpled form of the Kephi-boy on the platform, and she mutters, "Bullshit. Bullshit," over and over under her breath, and her eyes are full of tears. I didn't know she could do that, and I don't think she knew either.

And she's right. Big Tiny and his drugs have torn the soul

out of this nameless brat. The kid is a drooling idiot, and the ship is gonna take him to the back wards at Rockland State—if Big Tiny doesn't send him to the kingdom first.

The Kephi-boy is carried away to a small tent on the edge of the clearing. Big Tiny is still talking, but we've stopped listening. Margo is sitting on the grass, her head resting on her drawn-up knees. She looks pale and flushed at once. I ask her if she wants to try to check out the tent with me—see if the keph to feed the boy is there.

She says, "No. Leave me alone."

I remind her gently that all this was her idea. She tells me to go fuck myself. I figure I better check it out anyway. Big shot Faber.

"Wait here," I tell her, as if she looked like she was about to do anything else. The crowd is busy, on its knees, praying for candy canes or something. I slip around the edge of the mob. The boy's tent seems unguarded.

I'm by the entrance flap, hand on the canvas, when Petersen comes out of the shadows behind the tent. In his hand is a Browning automatic pistol—pointed at my stomach.

"Petersen, you're making me nervous. Put that thing away." And I'm thinking of my revolver sitting peacefully in my pocket. Do I pull it out and get myself killed? Petersen doesn't give me the opportunity. His gun doesn't waiver.

"I can save you the trouble of crawling around in there, Faber. Tiny dresses the boy in dolphin skin, and it stinks. Besides, you wouldn't be interested. There hasn't been any keph for the boy for three months now. Tiny's fresh out. He

knows the boy is a fizzle, like all the others. That isn't the
reason he's determined to get that box. He needs something heavy when it comes trading time, like everyone
else. He wants to build a hotel here. Big Tiny's Fontaine-
bleu, I imagine. He feels unprepared for the tourists, who
he expects momentarily. Ah well...every leader needs
purpose."

"I'd like to see the boy. Reporter's curiosity."

"The boy? He's sleeping, or in a coma. Probably got a
number of brain lesions and who knows what else. His diet
wasn't very regular. Take a look."

The boy is sleeping on a canvas cot. His breath comes hard,
as if his lungs were twisting inside his chest. The Nikon
kamoro is hanging on a tentpole above him, and I can see all
of his face. Up close, it's like a monkey's or a very old man's.
He is the most pitiful sight I have ever seen.

I turn away and squat there in the dark, in the stink of
fish, the sound of chanting, with Petersen impatiently
pacing across the front of the tent. I fantasize kidnapping
the boy, picking him up under one arm, rushing past
Petersen and his gun and the mob of crazy cultists—and
there we'd be: one big happy family. Margo, Faber, and the
Kephi-boy, at home in New Jerusalem, a world about to
end.

The insanity of it appeals to me, but not enough. I walk
out of the tent, and Petersen calmly waves goodbye, the gun
still steady in his other hand.

I find Margo in the crowd where I left her, slip my hand
under her arm, lift her up.

"Let's get out of here." She puts up no resistance, walks

along with me like someone stepping out of a car that's been
in an auto accident, unmarked, someone else's blood on her,
blank and dazed.

DURING THE MONSOON

What should we do but sing His praise
That led us through the wat'ry maze,
Unto an isle so long unknown,
And yet far kinder than our own....
—Andrew Marvell, *Bermudas*

I drop Margo at her place and head for the Blue Spruce
Motel, Sir Rodney's temporary headquarters. If there's
something live in that package Sir Rodney got from Wu
Fang, and he hung onto it and gave Runme a facsimile, I
should come into something. I figure I'm in the game now,
and keeping a reporter quiet shouldn't come too cheap.

The Blue Spruce is like a 1930's auto court in Florida.
One auto, Sir Rodney's ancient Rolls Royce. An Old
Wishing Well for atmosphere. A row of thin wooden doors.
On them, paintings of trees in blue. A sudden rattling noise
behind me: it's the motel's wooden signboard, slapping
against its post in a rising wind. The place looks deserted.
The wind gusts again, like a rough warm breath across my

face. The sky is roofed over completely with cloud, and darkening, though it's mid-afternoon.

I start at one end of the motel and knock on every door. I'm down to the last one, and imagining Sir Rodney's moved again and I'll never find him, when a door in the middle of the row opens. Miyoko Yakimoto sticks her head out and whistles. I go in.

Sir Rodney sits on the bed. Flies, a smell of some kind of disinfectant. A shoebox, wrapped in newspaper and tied with string, is enthroned on the pillow. Miyoko locks the door behind me. Sir Rodney gestures me to an orange vinyl armchair. He strokes his moustache.

"Stop your presses, Faber! Tell the world Sir Rodney Blessington has done his bowing and scraping—the last of it. Tomorrow morning we'll be aboard ship, and my story is perfect. It's obvious, don't you think? The pirate Wu Fang made the switch on Runme Singh. I'm just the faithful messenger boy."

Sir Rodney forces a laugh and it comes out ugly. He touches the box with nervous fingers.

"Here, within this box, lie film studios, young bodies male and female, leather easy chairs, dusty bottles of Armagnac, all wrapped neatly in newspaper, tied with string...."

His hands are shaking. He undoes the string, strips the newspaper away. He removes the lid. A sound comes up from Sir Rodney's throat like the bleating of the damned when they get the message it's for keeps. He should have known. Wu Fang diddled him. The box is filled with sawdust—and a rose.

I mentally shrug my shoulders—never sure he had it anyway. Miyoko is cursing in a mixture of Japanese and English, banging her tiny fists against the room's fake wood panelling.

Sir Rodney, however, is a broken man. He stands, shaky at first, then steadies himself. Tears are streaming down his face, dripping off his moustache onto his plum colored dressing gown. He sings softly through his tears. . . .

"Oh Danny boy. . .the pipes. . .the pipes are calling. . . ."

Until this moment, his opinions have managed to hold him together: the natural nobility of the Englishman, the auteur theory, the Queen's sexual excesses, the virtues of bear-baiting, the heroism of Ralph Roister-Doister, the innocence of John Profumo. But now, Sir Rodney's going down for the last time. The pirate outswindled him in a keph deal, the motel bill is probably unpaid, and Nanny died long ago. Only Miyoko remains.

"Miyoko, my girl, my blue. . .it's all a jest. . .into the void we flop, weeping. Even the tears of the dinosaurs as they watched their cozy cottages engulfed by glaciers can't match our own, eh?"

Rain begins to beat against the windows of the Blue Spruce Motel. Sir Rodney lies sobbing on the cheap yellow bedspread. The toilet of the motel room is clogged with sawdust. He has torn the rose to pieces with his teeth. He screams that he wants to die. He is no longer waiting for the ship, for the end, for his parachute to rise up from where he buried it twenty years ago and take him back up into the sky. He's quiet now—all his sins wash away in the early rains of the monsoon. His mind begins to darken, veiled by

the cloak of the fisherman. Miyoko is stroking his forehead.
He looks up.

"Miyoko, my girl, take me out to the Old Wishing Well.
I've wasted my life and now I'm done...."

He stands, puts one arm heavily over Miyoko's shoulder.
She leads him toward the door. Miyoko opens it, holds it
open with one arm. Sir Rodney turns back to me, his voice
unnaturally loud, to carry over the sound of the rain.

"Mr. Faber, you are a reporter." I nod. Sir Rodney takes
a long pause.

> My last words, before I pass.
> Hoist the bottle and kiss my ass.

Out the door they go, it banging shut in the wind behind
them. A moment, and I hear a sudden cry, as if of surprise,
and then, in a voice dying away, like that of someone falling,
falling, Sir Rodney cries, "Faaaaaade to blaaaaaack!"

An enormous splash—and silence.

I step out into the rain. Miyoko sits on the lip of the well,
dreaming of America.

I'm getting soaked, so I go back inside the motel room.
Hanging up over the bed, framed under cracked glass, is an
article torn from the Manchester Guardian twenty years
ago. A blurry photo of Sir Rodney as a young man and an
interview with him on yellowing newsprint. I quote:

> I refuse to waste the valuable time of my discerning audience
> with anything they can peep through their neighbor's
> window. I am an artist in film because the image is flat as a
> board, lantern slides from the land of the dead. I'm con-
> sistently amused by the hollow feeling that slides over me

when I complete a project that fills people's otherwise empty hours.

Miyoko is in the doorway, dripping, red silk kimono plastered to her body. Then her arms are around me, crotch bumping my thigh, hands flying over my back and ass. She's in a big hurry for something. She starts opening my fly, and she's just about got to where she's going, when I slow her down. I grab both wrists and hold them up in the air.

She decides not to kick me. Her breath is whistling in and out of her. She blinks at me, like she's remembering who I am.

"You can let me go now," she says, and I do it. She takes a step back.

"Sir Rodney is dead. I can be useful, even to someone from the outside."

I don't know what to do or say, so I stand there. I guess it looks to her like I don't believe her. She points a finger between her small breasts under the wet red silk. Her finger taps her breastbone.

"Fifteen things Miyoko can do at once: fuck anyone with an embarrassing amount of energy; exercise kidneys internally; listen to malicious gossip; laugh at bad jokes; concentrate on my expanded body theory—'I am you, so shut up and listen'; tap dance; worry about return of mother from radioactive ash—spanking; dream my guardian spirit— a three headed tortoise, six inches overhead in a cloud of juju dust; dig for tasty grubs in rotted log—survival skill; organize tomorrow's shooting schedule; rewire old walkie-talkies to create radio leak in the Ring of Fire; wiggle loose tooth right side bottom with my tongue; train ink monkeys; fart beautifully and strongly; replay old movies, frame by frame, on the inside of my skull."

Miyoko winks at me. She uncoils the red silk from around her body, standing there naked, except for the mother-of-pearl combs in her hair. She clears the bed, the pages of Sir Rodney's shooting scripts, timetables, brushes some of the sawdust of the phony keph to the floor.

More trouble than I need. I back toward the door. She lies naked on the bed, her legs open, looks at me as I step out into the rain. As I close the door to the motel room behind me, I can hear her screaming.

Along the curb, a row of rickshaws and pedicabs waits. The drivers are huddled together under the overhang of the Blue Spruce's roof, shooting craps. I tap a loser on the shoulder. He hops onto the little seat of a bike that hauls a passenger compartment enclosed on three sides. I pile in. It smells of old perfume in there, and some kind of sweet tobacco.

The cabman leans back, his red beard wet with rain.

"Well?"

For a moment I have no idea what he means. He's patient and he clarifies.

"Where you going?"

For lack of anything else in my head, I tell him the truth. "I don't know." Redbeard suggests that considering the monsoon is rising in New Jerusalem, and the whole damn place is folding up tomorrow morning, and specially since he gets paid for his time, it might be a good idea if I made up my mind.

"Take me to a nice high cliff," I tell him. He wants to

know if I'm trying to be funny. I say I'm not sure, and then I say, "Head for the Cockpit Hotel."

We're rolling, old rubber bicycle tires over cobblestones and mud, the labored breathing of Redbeard at the pedals. Wind slaps against the little oiled paper windows of the cab. We pass by the single landing strip of the New Jerusalem airport, then the low terminal building that serves as the control tower, a loudspeaker mounted on the roof.

The place reminds me of my arrival on the island, and it seems almost certain that I landed here many years before. Remembering the outside takes a strong effort of will. At the moment, I give up. I'm here—whenever I came.

The control room window is lit, and I can see a man in a moth-eaten Philadelphia Phillies baseball cap checking the instruments, talking softly into a throat microphone. Must be McPeak, the communications technician. I tell Redbeard to stop a moment. I lean out of the cab, peer into the window through the rain.

McPeak has torn the centerfold out of an old copy of *Loving Couples* and taped it up over his desk, scrawled across it in grease pencil, "Sweet Enough To Die For." It's a nude photo of a girl who resembles Margo, as she might have looked three or four years ago. She's sucking her thumb, and her forearm angles down between her breasts. She winks down at the top of McPeak's cap as his voice resumes its low drone. It whispers out of the roof speaker.

"Wind velocity 44, temperature 89.2 steady, barometer 9.9 and falling."

McPeak pauses, takes a swig of Green Spot, and wanders

over to the window, looking out toward us. At that moment, lightning, that lights up his silhouette like a scarecrow.

We roll, over the narrow strip of yellow light from the window on the wet concrete, and McPeak is gone. We're pedalling parallel to the blue flares along the landing strip now, and I spot two or three patient Kamoros huddled under a tarp. Airport watch duty. Maybe something will fly over, and if you aren't there to dance it down, you'll miss out again—so you sit there in the rain, ears tuned for the high drone of an approaching jet, water trickling down your collar, eyes blinking in the glare of the landing strip lights.

Redbeard doesn't falter, and we move on, streets deserted. Thunder—the monsoon is nearing its height. Back to the hotel before my meeting with Runme at the theatre. Maybe he's got the goods somehow after all. See Margo later. . . .

For one moment the hot wind pauses, and then a fresh breeze off the sea, cooler, breaks in over me. I shiver for a moment, wet with rainwater and sweat. I'm liking the rain. It's washing me somehow, settling the dust of New Jerusalem. . . .

We pass the corner of Change Alley, and the New Jerusalem Museum. There's Quang T. Lee, squatting in the doorway between two marble pillars, a kerosene burner alongside him. He's got the words "MUSEUM CLOSED" painted on the door in English, French and Arabic, and now he's working on the Japanese. He's got a brush full of black in one hand, and is trying to do a dignified museum-type job, his last task as assistant curator. It ain't easy in this weather. The shutters of the museum are flapping evilly around him, and soon the spirits in the wind and rain will rob him of his senses.

Redbeard slows down and my eye fixes a moment on the glare of orange flame through the side slits of the kerosene burner. Quang is curled up now, back to the door, and the wet paint above his head drips and smears in the driving rain. Monsoon at the museum door. Quang Lee's body rocks slightly as he chants, softly and steadily, to keep the wind demon out of his heart.

I spot the sputtering neon of the Cockpit Hotel in the distance, and lean back in the cab. Fantasy of Wu Fang in the monsoon fills my head. He's in a plastic submarine, fifty fathoms down below the Black Bastard, at the dead bottom of New Jerusalem harbor. Dolphins glide by. Wu Fang smiles at his lieutenant. He plays a card, the ace of hearts. A speaker behind them jerks with static. "Winds at seventy miles per hour northeast, waves thirty to forty feet and building...."

"It always strikes me as unusual," says Wu, "that this turbulence above—is not reflected below...."

Reverie cut by Redbeard's voice demanding the fare. We've stopped in front of the iron gate of the Cockpit Hotel. I pay up, run into the shelter of the lobby. The place feels like the set for a movie about a hotel, finished shooting years ago. Silence. Everything of value stripped away. Dust.

I wander up to my room and take off my wet clothes. The rain has stopped, but I'm sure it's only for a moment. The monsoon's got strength left to spend before it blows itself out. I go out on the terrace, figure I'll take a look at my fellow tenant's windows—see if he's at home.

I see the man himself. Petersen is on his balcony across the courtyard, silhouetted by his lit windows. A martini is on the stone railing in front of him. He's in his suit and tie again, the Kamoro get-up gone. He doesn't see me, as my room light is off, and it's already dusk. Petersen stares up at the frightful sky, the pale moon appearing and disappearing in great black sails of cloud. I can hear what sounds like radio static from the room behind him. Above there are no stars, and the wind whirls about New Jerusalem. Petersen kneels down now, as if in prayer, hands together on the railing, the light from his room bathing his back through the thin curtains. He stands, finishes his martini, tosses the glass into the courtyard below. He goes inside, closing the shutters behind him.

Changing into my dry suit for my meeting with Runme Singh at the theatre, I tie my tie, sit down on the rumpled bed, looking over the notes for my story. A knock at the door, and I know who it's got to be.

"Get outta here, Petersen. I'm busy."

"Faber!" he calls back through the door. "I've got some news you'll want to hear."

What the hell. I go to the night table, slip the Colt into my coat pocket. I don't think I got anything he wants, but you can't be sure. I open the door. Up close, Petersen looks haggard. His eyes are red. Whatever he's been doing, he's been hard at it. In his hand is a small shortwave radio.

"The ship's on the way, Faber. It'll be right on time in

the morning. Thought you'd want to hear Gabriel's trum-
pet, so to speak."

He sets the radio on the table, fiddles with dials.

Static, then a voice, suddenly clear. "North, northeast,
bearing 450, New Jerusalem weather conditions lousy,
visibility near zero. Should be clearing by morning. United
Nations Security Transport number one oh one over."

Static. Petersen fiddles again with the dials. Then:

"All troops. This is the captain speaking. There will be no
card playing on deck between 0900 and 1500 hours. All
weapons are to be cleaned and checked, full ammuniton
rations drawn from stores before morning. Weather should
be clear by 0400...."

The monsoon is screwing up the reception. More static.
The radio crackles and hums. It jumps a few inches off the
table as lightning strikes nearby. Then it's silent through
the slow roll of thunder. "Tuned in to their onboard
intercom," Petersen says. The radio crackles again.

"Orders are clear. If the prisoners are not waiting at the
dock, we will round them up. We are bringing them
freedom, and no trouble is anticipated. If any do resist
removal from the island, we will employ whatever force is
necessary. There are no weapons of any account in New
Jerusalem, so that, in any case, this is a pleasure cruise.

"There is to be no looting and no fraternizing. Our job is
to bring these people back safely and securely—if they are
salvageable. They haven't seen anyone from the outside
world for some time. We might seem strange to them. They
might seem strange to us. Be alert...."

Static, then silence. Petersen shakes the radio. Then he flips it off.

"Right on time, eh?" he says. Petersen takes a seat on the bed. He's making himself right at home. He clears his throat.

"Faber, tomorrow is going to be...hectic, and so is tonight. I just want to tell you something before I go." And all of a sudden Petersen is making me sicker than usual. I don't want to hear any of his deals or schemes or threats—or information.

"Petersen," I tell him, "I don't want to have anything the hell to do with you, understand? Why don't you just get out?" The answer surprises me.

"Faber, this is personal, that's all. There's no one else on this goddamn island I can talk to...they're different from us...and after tonight, I don't know what'll happen. Just listen to me, and I'll go."

I straighten my tie in front of the mirror. "I'm listening." Petersen leans forward on the bed, hands together, elbows on his knees.

"My first wife, Faber...she was the only person in this life I ever loved. I was lucky, and she married me. I was good looking then, years ago. For awhile I was happy. And then she got involved with another guy. I was working late on the paper. She was younger than I was. An old and simple story. Except this guy was trouble.

"I'll tell it quick. She ended up stabbing him in an argument. She was sent to New Jerusalem for life. I married again, had three kids, but I never loved any other woman in the same way.

"A few weeks ago I learned that my first wife had been

dead for almost a year, killed in a fight in some nightclub here. I traveled halfway around the world, to this insane little island, to put flowers on her grave. That was why I begged for this assignment from my editor. I begged him. He thought I was crazy.

"Now I'm here. I found that no one in New Jerusalem knows where she's buried. Funny, hah? Or maybe they know, and they won't tell someone from outside. What do you think, Faber? You think I'm a sentimental asshole?"

"No," I say. "I don't think that." Petersen stands up, picks up his radio. Confession's over, and he's back in business.

"Now that I'm here, there are, needless to say, other possibilities. Page one, this little place, don't you think? And Faber—I understand you. Believe me, I understand you."

Petersen's grinning at me from the doorway, like something's funny, like I'm at a party and my fly's open.

"I was you, once. Pawing around in the dark. It's sweet, really. Whatever happens here in New Jerusalem, Faber, I forgive you. In advance. Do you understand now?"

Petersen steps quickly out the door. I hear his footsteps fade down the hallway...roll of thunder, crackle of the short wave...clink of glasses in the empty bar..."Ink monkey, sahib?"

I turn up my jacket collar, check my pockets: notebook, pen, gun. I take out the revolver. It doesn't seem like anything less than a death ray is gonna do much good in this town, but I swing out the cylinder and put a sixth cartridge in the empty chamber I usually carry under the hammer. I slip it back into my pocket, safety off. I might shoot myself in the leg, but at the moment, that seems relatively unimportant.

I walk down the stairs, through the empty lobby, fishing canoe, potted palms, out through the iron gate, into New Jerusalem's final night.

AT THE THEATRE

Only a fool seeks the black smoke,
when the jackals sit in a ring.
—Sax Rohmer, *Dope*

The National Theatre of New Jerusalem is a huge circular shed left over from Arnheim's zeppelin project. It is dimly lighted by one enormous chandelier, suspended in its exact center. There are tiers of old red velvet theatre seats with chewing gum stuck underneath, popcorn vendors and hot dogs, an atmophere that is a cross between seedy grand opera and a South American soccer match.

Runme Singh's box ain't hard to find. A gilded tower sits alone at the edge of the stage, forming a front row of its own. A ladder runs up the back, and I climb it. I'm greeted at the top by two of Runme's goons with machine guns. Runme beckons me through.

There's only one chair in Runme Singh's box, and he's in it. The two guards stand behind him, and I stand alongside.

Runme's chair is plush and gilt, carved with fat cherubs in compromising positions. His yellowing fingers hold the package from Sir Rodney, a shoebox, wrapped in newspaper and tied with string. He balances it on his pointy knees.

The house lights begin to do a sixty second fade. I look around. Everyone is here. It's opening and closing night at once. Runme's council members in seedy tuxedoes with whores on their arms, amulet-sellers, peasants, vaqueros, butchers, falconers with their birds, flower-sellers, fishermen, janitors—from every quarter of New Jerusalem they come. Last show.

House lights out. Cheering and applause in the darkness. Then a white followspot picks up Runme in the box. I step back out of the glare. Runme stands, slipping the shoebox under his seat. He speaks to his people, raising his arms high.

"This evening's Tourist Promotion Board production at our National Theatre is *The History of New Jerusalem from Its Founding to the Present*, an original historical drama by New Jerusalem's poet laureate, Babu Grish Chunder Ghosh, written especially for our colony's final night of existence. This spectacle is no stale tale told in dull dialogue. The great statesman and visionary Arnheim will be revealed to you by a truly histrionic pen! His dying speech will bring a bubble into your heart! The drama's intention is to leave marks in the mind of the spectator, never to be erased. As for our scenic grandeur, I need only advise you to watch the performance with both eyes open."

Stage lights up. They reveal a thickly bearded man standing at a small table with alembics and crucibles. Allegorical Arnheim. Suddenly a peal of thunder from the monsoon outside helps out the dramatic moment. It also shakes the place. Damn close one. The actor playing Arnheim can't help grinning.

In his hand he holds an hourglass. After consulting it, he waves a wand. A good-looking fairy rises up from the floor and gives him a ring about the size of a doughnut. He waves his wand again and the fairy disappears. Throughout these proceedings a dark figure has been sleeping, unnoticed, toward the rear of the stage. A spotlight hits him, and a kick from the Arnheim magician brings the figure to his feet in apparent confusion. He bows, introducing himself to the audience as a half-witted Abyssinian slave named Aminadab. This character plays a part, totally irrelevant and absurd, in every succeeding scene.

The fact is that in New Jerusalem the audience demands the inclusion of this character in every play, no matter what the subject matter or style. If he's not present in each scene they begin yelling for him, so that the production has to come to a halt until he appears. It was soon discovered to be simpler if he was always on stage. The fabric of drama in New Jerusalem is strained somewhat by this practice. Aminadab always combines comic stupidity with a great love of creature comforts, and spends his time in obscene mockery of everyone else in the play.

Next Scene: A giant paper mâché dog enters, and litters three men. They have the heads of lizards and large square teeth. They come out squealing, snap and tear at each other. Then they rip their paper and paste mother to pieces.

Two other figures appear stage front, a British University lecturer and a sexy American high school student in cut-offs.

Lecturer: What you see is, I believe, an allegory of the founding of the city of New Jerusalem. The three figures represent....(looks at watch). Excuse me, darling. I have a class. (He exits.)

Student (to audience): Travel is so exciting, and even if we all can't do it, learning about faraway places and the customs of other people is so nice....

At this point in her burbling, a hideous giant Chinaman enters in a green robe. He picks her up under one arm, without breaking stride. He is dragging behind him a toy duck on a string. The duck has big yellow wheels and is quacking. Follow spot on duck. Blackout.

Runme loves every moment. He leans over the railing of his private box, banging his hands together. He turns back to me.

"That writer has a way with words. Makes them do anything he wants. Like you, Faber. Our newspaper on the outside...powerful...." I just nod in the dark. He's excited, and he's rambling.

"Who was that actress? Must try to find her on the ship...my compliments...." There's a lull in the onstage action, and Runme sits back. He runs his hands over the shoebox in his lap. He can't wait. Old fingers begin to grope at the knot, voices of the actors in his ears.

The cast launches into a complex dance recalling Arnheim's spiritual birth pangs. Slow going. The audience begins to fart and cough, fight among each other. Somebody in a back row yells something at the stage. The second act is bogging down.

Suddenly the stage revolves, the dancers being carried away behind the scenes. They look surprised. One of them yells, "Hey! What the hell's...," but his complaint about the director's artistic judgment is overwhelmed by another sudden crack of thunder.

The new scene that revolves into view has the stage divided into three compartments. Stage left, a mechanical figure representing Arnheim stands in a booth. He hands a row of original natives of the island small pieces of paper. A sign over the booth reads: "TICKETS TO HEAVEN."

Center stage, a man in a white linen suit is busily setting fire to a large wooden model of an old B-52 bomber, which hangs in the air above the stage.

Stage right, the actor who played Arnheim in the first scene stares upward through binoculars from a mock-up of a stone terrace. His lines are: "There she goes, honey-pie. Let's get those development plans out and go to work."

These three scenes run simultaneously and continuously, over and over, like a film loop. After ten minutes the audience is twitching badly. This sequence is a bust, to say the least. A fat couple demanding their money back shoulder their way up the aisle. Tomatoes begin to hit the stage.

Runme Singh doesn't notice. He no longer sees anything but the box on his lap. He begins undoing the string. His hands are shaking. He whispers under his breath.

"Showers of uncut keph...membership in interlocking

directorates of media corporations...buy a senator or
two...easy street...."

Onstage the play within a play portion of the evening
begins, a chronicle of Runme's exploits specially inserted by
Narduke Pemmican, Runme's speechwriter, a hopeless
drunk who published a promising first novel before he
began his career as a forger. This segment stars New
Jerusalem's matinee idol, Tipton Spoke, as Runme, plus the
Lunn sisters, who are real lookers, plus a chorus of dancers
costumed as hideous representatives of the Kamoro cult.

I look over the chorus line. They're busy doing high
kicks, and the identical prop kamoros they wear are painted
with the faces of demons. They stop kicking and twirl about.
There are lots of them, filling the stage. The Kamoro cult is
not really subject to satire. There's no way to exaggerate
their behavior, so you end up with an imitation, in which it
would be easy to conceal the real thing....

In fact, one dancer, particularly awkward, on the end of
the line, looks familiar. Then I realize it's Harry the Horse,
same costume as the others, but not quite as familiar with the
routine. Trouble.

Runme, however, is staring down into his lap. The string
is undone, the dancers twirl, and outside the National
Theatre the monsoon is at its height. Thunder mingles with
the tremoloes and squeaks of the orchestra.

The box of keph is a whirlwind spinning Rumme's
prayer wheel—fruit of twenty years of bribery and corruption in one neat package. The lid's off. Runme sticks one
fat finger into the red powder filling the box. He smears
some on his lips, on the inside of his left wrist, waits for the

keph stars to light up in his backbrain. He waits for the
blonde member of the Lunn sisters to turn into Mother
Teresa and his favorite whore.

Nothing. Runme shrieks.

"Johnson and Johnson baby powder and red food
coloring!"

His prayer wheel drifts to a stop, but he's still going.
"Who pulled the switch? Rodney? Leroy? Wu Fang? You,
Faber? You!"

He stands, staggers toward me. The play has stopped,
frozen. I back away, Runme's fingers groping for my
throat.

Harry the Horse leaps forward out of the chorus of
dancers onstage, rips off his demon kamoro, pulls a gun
from under his robe. He fires three shots into Runme's
back, pointblank range. Runme turns toward the stage,
stares at Harry out of dead eyes. He slumps down onto the
railing, bleeding into the yellow rug. One hand paws blindly
at the box of red dust, and it slips away from his nerveless
fingers.

The actors panic; the curtain falls. From the sky, an
enormous peal of thunder. The windows of the National
Theatre of New Jerusalem burst and the wind demon whirls
about the chandelier. The assassin disappears into the night.
Runme's body slides down to the floor of his gilded box. I
head for the exit.

The monsoon has ended as suddenly as it began. Gray
clouds scud across a brilliant moon, its hazy blue aureole
filtering out to the very ends of the sky. Here below,

everything is in relief, bright with moonlight. And the air is full of that lush after-rain smell, thick, almost rotten.

I wander aimlessly, putting some distance between me and the theatre, trying to clear the overload in my head. Sidewalks of New Jerusalem, after midnight. Violet glow of streetlamps. Empty arcades, wooden tables cleared of goods, the proprietors next to their wives and children, sleeping in the open or under a flap of canvas. An arm is thrown about a warm waist, voices whisper in their sleep—

"Kiss me, baby, so I know you're mine...."

"Heaven and hell together give me tingles...."

I step over a guy sleeping it off in the middle of the sidewalk. Then I see a little puddle of blood under his neck. Young man, average build, well-dressed, dead. Wallet and identification gone. Someone wants to be somebody else in the new world, when the ship comes in.

I stand in a doorway, wondering what next. No one passes by. The ship figures to arrive at dawn. I look at my watch. One A.M. I search anyway for that thin line of light along the horizon. Not yet, but I can stand here and dream it...white ghost of the Titanic easing over the water toward New Jerusalem. A detachment of U.N. prison guards plays cards below decks. Thompson submachine guns in a rack by the door. On the bridge, the Captain checks the instruments, looks out into the night. It's clear now, moonlight pretty on the waves. He sings a little childhood song to himself....

Uncle John is very sick, what shall we send him?
Three good wishes, three good kisses,
    and a slice of ginger....

His voice rises, echoes out over the calm sea.

Who shall we send it by? By the ferryman's daughter
Take her by her lily-white hand
and lead her over the water

I've seen a few of these switches now, and I'm getting
certain about who's got the button. I could buy myself a new
set of identification, and a newspaper in the bargain. Fire
the editor or shift him to latrine duty. I could be at the
Captain's table when that ship comes in.

I look out at the empty street. My head's clear. I got a
chance at the box, and I'm taking it. There are no rules in
New Jerusalem. I am here. Convicted. Dropped by parachute. Born here. This is my story now. I've got as much
right to it as any of them.

Got to pick up Margo, take her with me. I start running,
realize it's too damn far to her place, slow to a fast walk.
Need to find Wu Fang. On the Black Bastard or at that
temple Sir Rodney told me about.

This little world is steaming up before it shuts out. Big
Tiny is in an all-night prayer meeting, waiting for his
assassin's report, waiting for the ship to arrive and open its
doors, and golden peacocks with saxophones will proclaim
the arrival of everything they've seen in faded magazines,
and the tourists will rise up and coat the land with honey.
The dock must be already covered with offerings of flowers
and food...shooting schedule on an orange bedspread...
light glints off silver fingerguards...blood dark on the
yellow rug...I go around a corner, past Cowboy Dreamland. Lights out, door left open, flapping in the wind. No
need to lock up. Nobody home.

ABOARD THE
BLACK BASTARD

*Behold, I shew you a mystery; We shall
not all sleep, but we shall all be changed.*
—Corinthians I, 15:51

Margo runs alongside me, her hair flying back in the night air, breath coming easy, filling her small chest—steady lope. She thinks we better check the Luck and Virtue Temple for Wu Fang before heading out to the Black Bastard. Necessary stop. If we take the ferry and Wu's on shore somewhere, we might be too late. Once the U.N. ship arrives, no telling what might happen.

Margo knows where to find it—an old stone building sitting alone on a sidestreet near the docks, its outer garden overgrown with weeds.

The Temple of Luck and Virtue is the one building left standing from before the prison colony began, a reminder of the religion of the original islanders. Fishermen found a corpse floating in the sea near the spot where the temple now stands. The corpse was of a man, but a kind of man the islanders had never seen before. They made a tomb for the corpse and began to pray for its spirit. This practice spread until a temple was established on the spot.

The tomb of the floating corpse is still there, under a tree in the outer courtyard. Soil from the grave is believed to have healing powers, and has been used so extensively that the corpse is almost uncovered. In fact, one of its hands lies above the loose dirt of the grave, ivory fingers graceful and relaxed.

We pass through this outer courtyard and under a low stone arch. Beyond is an inner court. Incense, stone walls damp with moss. In one corner of this courtyard a shining white Mercedes convertible is parked, like something from another world.

Margo whispers "Bingo! We've come to the right place. That's Wu's car." I am still staring at it, wondering if it's real, when an old man in yellow robes appears, his round face peeping forward from under his hood, like an owl's. He walks toward us, speaks confidingly, as if we were all old friends.

"Pardon me. I don't wish to intrude, but I thought the two of you would be interested to know that it is on the design of this very temple that the obscene corridors of Arnheim's destroyed Maze Palace were based. Ironic, isn't it? I have ceased to find it so, after being here so long. I stopped teaching, you know, years ago. I found I wasn't sure enough about anything to guide others. They find their way well enough without me. Now, I catch toads for soup, and make chitchat with visitors very like yourselves."

The monk links one arm in mine, and one in Margo's. He's between us, and turns us in a slow circle as he speaks, as if to give us a complete view of the inner court.

"The warmer air here, Mr. Faber, clogs the left nostril of the novices. Uncomfortable at first. The fire dakinis are rose-madder, rather than the crimson they appear further north. In this case, the absence of resources from the outside—communications, transportation, and climate control in particular—which absence we usually find beneficial—is troublesome. We'd install a Carrier Frostbite Unit, if one was available. The postulant should occasionally be able to see his breath, even in New Jerusalem."

I'm surprised. First man on the island who thinks they're better off than the outside, with more of an open field. But I'm too impatient to let him go on.

"Did you happen to see a certain Wu Fang this evening?"

"Certainly. Mr. Fang is one of our regular devotees." The monk gestures to a squat servant who had been crouched in a corner. The man moves rapidly off toward the central hall, banging his rosewood clappers.

"I hope you and the young lady find your wait for Mr. Fang to be not without interest. The temple is extensive and the search for this person may take some hours. Please feel free to use our library...files of the *Reader's Digest*, ancient stone tablets, complete Dickens...."

We wait. Margo wanders off somewhere, and I begin to stare at a painting, high up on the temple wall. It is in shadow. The central figure seems to be a young girl, dressing for the prom before her mother's mirror. A double bed behind her is covered with a puffy green quilt. On the dressing table are perfumes, eye shadow, a Bible. She adjusts her bra cups about her breasts, raises her arms to drop a gold chain over her head. On the end of the chain a little sailing ship in shiny black enamel touches her warm skin, giving the slightest chill....

Five monks in yellow robes quickly enter the inner court, take up positions around Wu Fang's white Mercedes. They begin to polish it industriously, passing the can of Simonize from one to the other. Their chant of "Pass the Simonize" echoes into the night.

Then Margo is back alongside me, beckoning me to follow her. She walks through bronze doors leading to a very long and narrow hallway hung with cheap bead curtains. I'm right behind her. At the very end of this hallway Wu Fang sits in an overstuffed armchair. A forty-watt bulb swings aimlessly over his head. Flies. He is in a bathrobe, and around his neck is a five-and-dimer of a crucifix, with a gold painted Jesus on a cross of red plastic. A radio plays alongside him, a transmission that sounds like it might be a news story involving the closing of the island prison of New Jerusalem, the visit of a reporter, and what he finds there. The sound is blurred, the reception poor....

Margo steps aside to let me pass. Wu Fang stands up to greet me. He bows.

Walking with me in the quiet courtyard, Wu Fang is again in his black silk robe, clasped with coral. His skin seems polished like old ivory, and his green eyes shine. It is the dark middle of the night. He talks softly.

"Do you know the English painters, Mr. Faber? I collect them. It is instructive. Blake and Reynolds are my particular passions."

I just nod to let him know I'm listening. There's no use asking this man questions. He knows why I'm looking for him at three A.M., and he'll tell me what he'll tell me. We are both silent for a long moment. Then Wu Fang speaks again.

"All living things are of air, fire, earth and water—the five grains, the frog in his caved-in well, flying things—even those creatures who walk on two legs, with their teeth inside their mouths, hair on their heads, with hands different from their feet, that we call men. . . . Of them all, the dolphins— the dolphins made a wise choice.

"They developed lungs along with men, Mr. Faber, but then they held a conference along the shore. 'Must we live,' they said, 'on a small slice of the planet, build cities, and wet each other down with the spit of our tongues? No. We will return to the one sea, and live in it till we die.'

"The dolphins failed to anticipate the attitude of those who chose to remain on land. All we can find for them is envy. We spread death on the waters, steal the keph from their still twitching bodies.

"Now that we begin to know more, Mr. Faber, we may return. Back to high school. To grade school. We go to kindergarten. We go back to the sea. . . .

"Have you tried the keph, Mr. Faber? I have a rather large package of it on board the Black Bastard. Come with me, and we can wait on deck for the first lights of the liner, which, no doubt, we will see dimly, glimmering in the mist. . . ."

Margo's eyes are bright. She's been listening, and she's quick. We could share it, or steal it, or he'll give it away. She's thinking we have a chance. So am I.

Margo gets in the back seat of the Mercedes. I get in front, and Wu Fang is behind the wheel. He reaches toward the ignition key, then stops, looks over at me. His long silver fingerguards brush my sleeve.

"You're becoming like a friend of mine, Faber. An old friend. Hua Tzu, the fisherman. When he reached middle-age he suddenly lost his memory. If he received anything in the morning, he forgot all about it by the evening; if he gave anything away at night, he forgot all about it by the next day. He forgets to walk or to sit down. He forgets today the events of yesterday, and by tomorrow he will have forgotten all about today...."

Deserted boulevards, narrow sidestreets. No other cars. Wu drives very fast. He is silent. I look in the rearview mirror. Margo is lighting a cigarette. Her eyes are shining like a cat's in the back seat. On the tufted leather behind her, a design of a phoenix, tooled in gold.

We pull up by a shabby pier. Wu drives the Mercedes into a battered garage made out of coca-cola signs. Alongside the pier sits a black outrigger canoe, manned by four of Wu's pirate crew. The three of us get on board. The single lantern of the Black Bastard lies like a low star on the horizon. The pirates chant steadily in a language I do not understand, as their paddles dig deep into the waves.

Two red lights, high off the water, come up fast behind us. A roar of powerful engines. Our crew strokes for all they're worth, but it's a joke. Whatever it is, it's doing about forty knots, and gaining fast. The night is clear, and in a minute I can make it out—if I couldn't hear its engines, I'd be sure I was hallucinating. The damn thing looks like an enormous sea-snake, it's flat reptile head rising from the water, with scaly sides, a pointed tail that curves up over the stern. The red gleams are its eyes. It's close, and throws on searchlights. The beams are blinding. Then the world is filled with the roar of its engines. It cuts us off, and we rock in its wake as it backs slowly toward us.

"One of Arnheim's original devilboats," Wu Fang murmurs. "I haven't seen one in twenty years." As I get a better look at it, I remember what I'd read in one Tourist Promotion Board guidebook—Chris-craft Comanches with a fiberglass overshell designed to look like a giant sea-snake. They were built by Arnheim to discourage the natives of nearby islands from attempting to trade or even explore the waters around New Jerusalem. Contamination by the "outside." The boats have been in storage for years, but someone must have gotten the key.

I don't need to guess who that someone is. Petersen appears, leaning over the devilboat's stern. The crew of the crazy Chris-craft are massed behind him: Kamoros, about fifty of them. They sway back and forth, some staring at us, others looking in the other direction, out across the water, for the first glimpse of the great ship of the gods. The helmsman of the devilboat is particularly distracted, staring up at the sky. The Kamoros have lost any grip they ever had on reality with the approach of their apocalypse, and it must be all Petersen can do to have them run the ship. Now, engines cut off for the moment, it drifts aimlessly alongside us.

Petersen, however, is alert as ever. In one hand he holds a bullhorn, and in the other is a light machine pistol. Very ugly weapon. I look over at Wu Fang. His eyelids are peeled back like a snake's. My name booms at us over the bullhorn.

"FABER! This is our water meeting! First air, then land, now water. What's left? Think about it." Petersen pulls the trigger, lets off a three-second burst. Fucking machine-pistol. Half the side of our canoe splinters away. One of the pirates holds onto his thigh, and I see the blood coming through his fingers. He falls over into the bottom of the canoe. The bilge slops with water and blood.

"FABER!" I look down at the corpse. His mouth lies open and a gold tooth shines.

"FABER!" again on the bullhorn. The boats are about ten yards apart now. Petersen speaks slowly, concerned that I follow every word.

"I've done my homework, Faber. Either you or Wu Fang has the keph, or it is lost, or it does not exist. I choose not to believe in the latter two alternatives. You, I assume, still retain some moral objections to this sort of carrying on. Even if you could, you wouldn't hurt me unless it was necessary. As you can see, I have effectively stripped away the fabled thin veneer of so-called civilization, so that I am in the enviable position of not giving a shit whether I kill you or not. The keph, Faber! Hand it over!"

I shout back across the water to the Chris-craft.

"Petersen! We don't have it!"

Petersen's response is quick. His voice is louder, more strained.

"If you don't have it, you're on your way to get it. What else would bring you out here in the middle of the night?"

Wu Fang answers him before I can think of anything bright to say.

"Boating," says Wu. He barely raises his voice, but it's clear, and I'm sure Petersen hears every word. "We are boating in New Jerusalem harbor. If you fail to revive within yourself the graciousness and courtesy to allow us to continue, unimpeded by yourself or your vessel, you will discover, to your everlasting regret, that on one day in the near future, due to the activites of myself, if I am spared to perform such actions, or my associates if I am not fated to direct your disposition in person, that you will be initiated into the mysteries of pain to an extent you cannot now imagine. It will take you weeks to die. Goodbye."

Wu gestures to his remaining pirates to paddle, and the result is that Petersen fires another burst across our bows. The pirates drop their paddles into the bay, cower down with their heads between their knees. Petersen shouts into his bullhorn again.

"I intend to search you."

Margo, who's been fairly steady up to now, slides up next to me, holds onto my arm. She's as scared as I am. Lines are thrown out from the Chris-craft, and a group of Kamoros haul us in to its side. Petersen steps down into the canoe, pokes his machine-pistol into my ribs. He looks everywhere.

"It must be aboard the Black Bastard then. We'll just go out there and tear that junk apart." He looks down at me and Margo, and he knows he's got it right this time. He's in charge, and he's crazy with it. He grins.

"Good story, Faber. Half for Big Tiny, half for me, and your corpse at the bottom of New Jerusalem harbor."

Maybe she looks at him funny, or maybe he's just nuts, but Petersen suddenly slams Margo across the face with his free hand. She falls backwards to the bottom of the canoe. The boat rocks and Petersen slips, off balance for a moment. I reach into my pocket, drag out the Colt. It seems to take years. I fire three shots into Petersen's face. Blood wells out of the holes in his forehead and cheek, and he topples over slowly into the bay. He sinks without a sound.

The Kamoros on the deck of the devilboat leap up and down, screaming and chanting. Wu Fang reaches down to where Petersen's machine-pistol fell into the slosh of blood and water on the canoe bottom. He wipes the gun dry on his robe. He stands up. When the Kamoros on the Chris-craft see him, they quiet down. He just stands there, pointing the barrel at them, and after a while they are simply staring back at him, like wide-eyed children in a nursery.

Wu Fang aims just below the waterline, and he holds back the trigger till the magazine is empty. One long burst, and a jagged hole opens in the devilboat's side, shards of fiberglass sprinkle the water. The devilboat begins to tilt, as the dark water of the bay fills her insides. The cult members rush to start her engines, and I can hear them sputter and die. Then the Kamoros begin to leap into the sea, screaming and floundering, slapping and kicking at the water. Their boat rears nose up, and goes under. Its searchlights are somehow still on, and we watch the yellow spots grow dimmer and smaller as they sink, until they wink out.

My arm is around Margo as we paddle slowly out toward the Black Bastard, and again I search the horizon for the first thin line of light. Not yet.

We sit cross-legged on a mat, on the deck of the Black Bastard, opposite Wu Fang. He has said nothing about the keph for an hour. I don't want to look eager—yet. I have stopped listening to him for a moment, drifting, and then Wu Fang's voice comes back to me.

"...and that is why," Wu Fang is saying, "the deer sleeps with his nose on his tail. Please print that story in your newspaper. If it is well received I have another, entitled 'The Fleshly Heart is Like a Peach.'" Toward the stern of the junk, Wu Fang's men are packing their gear, preparing to greet the dawn.

Suddenly, with a great hiss of escaping air, Arnheim's mechanical Chinese dragon rises sluggishly from the bay, about fifty yards from the Black Bastard. Wu Fang and I move over to the rail. Steam bursts from the creature's nostrils. His green-gold neck, trailing sheaves of fin and wing, rises forty feet into the air. Up this close I can see that on his back there seems to be pictured, in the pattern of the scales, a scene in which a giant turtle has filled a caved-in well with one foot, trying to get into it. The turtle is calm, in fact, amused. A small frog sits to one side, his eyes swollen out of his head in shock and horror. As the dragon sinks back into the bay, the thin blue line of dawn marks a great circle around us, between sea and sky.

Wu Fang talks softly, close to my ear. "Somewhere out on the ocean the ship approaches, the Captain sleeping in his cabin, soldiers playing cards below decks. On the docks of New Jerusalem, a few stray people gather, mostly prostitutes and peddlers who have misunderstood the news. Early cult members are strewing the quay with flowers, coating their kamoros with new paint.

"It is dawn. The Captain wakes, checks his position, flips the lever that deactivates the Ring of Fire. Around New Jerusalem the invisible seal crackles and sparks, then disappears. Sharp smell of ozone as the air without mingles with our air within. Can you smell it, Faber?

"Now you can imagine the white bulk of the liner breaking through the morning fog, much closer than you ever thought it would be at your first sight of it, its fog horn sudden, unbelievably loud and strong."

Mist rises off the warm harbor waters, first rays of the rising sun slant up through it to diffuse into the palest of pink froth on the air. Where the mist breaks, lines of red light stab through like lasers. I tear my mind back to what we came for. I've got to make my play. Exactly how, I don't know. But it doesn't matter. Wu Fang gets there first.

He bows, first to Margo, then to me. "Now, what you have been so patiently waiting for. What you have kept me company in the sleepless night for. What you no doubt saved my life for. Excuse me, please. I will return in a moment."

Wu Fang goes below. I finger the gun in my coat pocket. The other pirates aboard are lounging sleepily at the stern. The black canoe bobs at the end of its line. The morning mist grows thick. Margo's fingers are twisting together. She kisses me. Her lips are very sweet and hot, her arms tight around my neck. I run my hands over her back under the thin silk, holding her.

Wu Fang returns to the deck, carrying a shoebox wrapped in newspaper and tied with string. He looks at us together, and he cannot suppress a tiny smile.

"Now," whispers Margo in my ear, and she lets me go.

Wu Fang unties the box, lifts the lid. The keph is a deep crimson, like venous blood, and crystalline—tiny particles glowing like crushed fragments of fire-opal. Wu slides his silver fingerguards off the index and middle fingers of his right hand. They clatter to the deck. He pinches up a bit of the keph, squeezes the crystals to powder, lets the red dust drift from his fingers. A smell like the bottom of the sea soaks the air around us.

I take my gun out of my pocket, point it at Wu Fang. I say, "Give us the box." Margo holds out her hands for it, in a gesture that's more plea than demand. Wu is amused.

"Are you going to kill me, Mr. Faber?"

"I will if I have to. Give the package to her."

"To Margo? No. I did not give it to any of the others in New Jerusalem. I will not give it to you. The world outside will love the keph far more than we did. You will sell it there for money. They will want more when it's gone. They will use their modern scientific instruments, and rediscover the exact ingredients and method of manufacture. Then they will rape the oceans for the flesh they need.

"Kill me if you like. I doubt that any number of bullets in this body could prevent me from performing my last act in New Jerusalem as I intend."

In one sure movement, Wu Fang dumps the keph over the side. He pours it out in one steady crimson stream, its color mixing with the sunrise. Margo is laughing now, and she can't stop. I feel like a fool, holding the damn gun in my hand. I put it away. Wu Fang tosses the empty box over the side as well.

"Back to its source, Mr Faber. They are all gone now—Runme Singh, Sir Rodney, Dr. Leroy. Big Tiny is on the pier, waiting for the book of kings to be given him. He cannot read it. New Jerusalem is ended, and the higher paradise, where there is no keph, has not yet opened its doors. In the corridor between them, we labor.

"I choose to remain on the Black Bastard. My crew are taking the canoe to shore. If I am not mistaken, they all wish to go."

Out of the mist comes what seems at first to be a great iceberg, drifted down from the north. It glides toward the flimsy pier like a white dinosaur, twin streaks of rust along the waterline, black funnel with a red band. It dwarfs the island and all its creations. On the pier men begin to dance and moan. Dolphins are leaping in the waves around New Jerusalem, risen up to the morning light from where they lay on the bottom, dead or sleeping.

GOODBYE

"How many miles to Babylon?"
"Three score and ten."
"Can I get there by candlelight?"
"Yes, and back again."
—Children's rhyme

The ocean liner glides into the quay so slow...time stop. The Kamoro cultists on the pier are frozen in awe. Big Tiny's mouth is open—a butterfly could land on his tongue, its wings colored windows in the air. Giant sheets of white steel shear upward over them in an impossibly graceful curve. The ship stops, a gentle wake dies, and it floats on an unbroken sea of glass.

Nothing moves. Margo and I pull chairs over to the rail of the Black Bastard. I take out my notebook. We've got the best seats in the house.

No human figures appear on the liner's deck. Quiet. The Kamoro cult crowds the pier, mobs of them on the neighboring docks, filling the nearby streets. Some are up on the roofs of warehouses. Piles of fruit, crocodile hides, flowers.

And then a giant white loudspeaker, mounted on the liner's deck, glides along its steel track, clicks in to its receiving slot at the prow. In position, the speaker swivels till its bell is pointed toward the interior of the island, and the city of New Jerusalem. It crackles into life with a sound like the voice of God. The people on the pier sink to their knees.

From out here on the Black Bastard I can hear the damn thing perfectly. It seems to gain a sharpness coming over the water. Wu Fang squats on his mat, reading the philosopher. He's uninterested in all this, as if he already knows the outcome. Margo is staring at the ship like a kid at Christmas. Keph or no, she's ready for the world. It's shiny.

The speaker is clearly (to me, at any rate) running a pre-recorded tape, made to be played at the moment of the ship's arrival by a professional actor, hired by the United Nations for his comforting and reassuring voice—his warmth.

Deep Man's Voice Over Ship's Speaker: "People of New Jerusalem, convicts and the children of convicts: yours is a sorrowful history. You have served as an experiment in penology for fifty years, and served well. That experiment need not be evaluated. It is obsolete. This island is no longer needed. Today, New Jerusalem, as you have so ironically named your place of incarceration, is officially closed. We welcome you back to the world.

"You will be treated well, and integrated completely into our society. Homes are waiting. Employment is waiting. Freedom is waiting.

"Drug rehabilitation and reconditioning treatment for those of you who require it will begin immediately aboard ship, as will the accompanying motor and mental tests. Welcome aboard."

A circular hatch opens like a metal flower in the ship's side. A wide white gangplank slides out and lowers to the dock. The Kamoro cult members just stand there. They have no way of understanding what they've heard—or they simply refuse to understand it. They do not move.

Non-cult citizens of New Jerusalem are nowhere to be seen, their view of the ship's arrival being far more matter-of-fact. They figured they have to leave their homes, jobs, and lives for something new, better or worse. "Let them come to us. When they do, O.K., we'll go," is the attitude. So while there's no business as usual in New Jerusalem, those who, along with Runme Singh, would not have been surprised by the loudspeaker announcement—were at home, calmly packing, and saying goodbye to one life in the face of another. Plenty of time. They didn't think the ship would leave without them.

On the pier, representing all of New Jerusalem to the eyes of the as yet invisible Captain and crew of the U.N. transport, is the Kamoro cult.

Someone throws one flower toward the ship. It lands in the water, between the wooden pier and the ship's steel side. It floats there, petals awash. Then Big Tiny starts to wail. It's a sound like none I ever heard before, floating over the water like the death sob of a banshee. I can see his big body twist and bend with the force of the noise, as it powers up through his chest from the dark of his belly and mind. In a moment

this monstrous keening is echoed back to him by the other
cult members on the quay. An enormous moaning, which
begins to be mingled with the names of the gods: "Sannyo.
Betamax. Magnavox! MAGNAVOX!"

I hear Wu Fang's voice from behind me. "Magnavox is
their god of retribution and anger." He joins us at the rail,
takes a long look.

"This is the opening of the final scene. You'll pardon my
interruption, but I only do so to indicate my own disgrace in
neglect of my guests. My crew is gone, meeting friends and
lovers before going to the ship, suitcases packed with antique
dimestore necklaces and paper money so worn that no one
can tell from which country it comes. I am alone. With your
assistance, we can bring this floating parcel of dog dung in
close enough to observe events with the proper combination
of detachment and interest."

I give him a hand with some rigging, though Wu Fang
seems perfectly capable of handling the junk alone. She
swings in toward shore. Margo keeps watch, and in a
moment she's shouting for me to join her. We drop anchor.

Men have appeared on the deck of the U.N. transport, in
the baby-blue combat uniforms of the United Nations
Prison Security Forces. They hold riotguns across their
chests, march with a determined step down the ship's deck.
I can tell by one look at them—they think they know where
they are.

"Alcatraz, Sing-Sing, New Jerusalem: same difference. A
prison's a prison."

I want to shout to them: "This is New Jerusalem! Those
people *live* here! They seem nuts to you, but . . ." and I know

it'll be just another lunatic yelling how he's not crazy from the back of the back wards. Besides, if I start yelling, whatever happens we'll be in it, and I'm getting damn sure that's not a good idea.

On the liner everything is still. The figures on its deck look like toy soldiers. On shore, the chanting of the cultists gains volume and emotion. One figure on deck steps forward, vigorously beckons them aboard. No one goes.

The prerecorded tape plays again, louder this time. "PEO-PLE OF NEW JERUSALEM, CONVICTS AND THE CHIL-DREN OF CONVICTS..." then switches to French, Swahili, Chinese.

From our floating vantage point we can see the first wave of citizens with suitcases, followers of the Tourist Promotion Board, who have packed and are prepared to leave. They walk up the dusty hill from the city toward the harbor—children, baggage, valuables. When they reach the top, they will see the ship, walk solemnly down to it and get on board. And those on the ship will see them. There's about three minutes before they reach the hilltop.

I understand Kamoro cult enough to guess what Big Tiny thinks is happening. He'll understand it all in a flash of insight. Those from outside on the ship have their treasures, but they will not turn them over to the faithful Kamoro cult, as the gods have instructed them to do. They will not give the signal to release the tourists from beneath the earth. They've made a deal with Runme Singh's ghost, or with Faber, the American.... If the Kamoro cult does not wish to once more have taken from them by men what the gods wish to give them, there is only one alternative. They must fight.

I figure it right. Big Tiny reaches down into the dust at his feet, takes up a stone. Old Bible phrase from ten years old lights up a split-second in my head. "Let he who is...." Tiny throws the stone at the ship. It clangs harmlessly against the metal hull. He reaches for another. The cult members around him get the idea. The deck of the ship is pelted with stones. One young U.N. soldier is hit, falls, blood streaming from his forehead.

Big Tiny's mouth opens like the mouth of hell. He shouts a command, language I don't understand. The Kamoro cult goes mad. Their tongues shoot out in unison, waggle like those of demons on old postcards. Drums. Stones and heavy pink fruit fly—gifts turn to weapons, squish against the white steel like runny wounds.

One tall man, wearing the rusted Leica of an obdurato, leaps into the water, attempts to scale the side of the ship. His nails rip as they attempt to dig into the metal, ten streaks of dull gray undercoat point down to his splashing body. A screaming mob—Hawaiian shirts, sunglasses, kamoros, golf hats, and all—hurls itself up the gangplank.

As they rush toward the open hatch, I can see the Captain peering at them through binoculars from the wheelhouse. "Madmen," he must be thinking, "the island is populated by madmen." He flips the retract lever for the gangplank. It begins to withdraw into the side of the ship as the cultists rush along it. They fall screaming into the water, as U.N. troops in baby-blue flak jackets fill the open hatchway. They wear blue plastic helmets, each of them with a riotgun that must fire fifty rounds a second.

They hold their fire, the Kamoro cultists falling helplessly into the bay. One of them lets off a warning burst into the water next to the pier. The splashes the slugs make wet the bottom of Big Tiny's robe. He begins to speak in tongues, his jaws flapping open and shut like a switch on overload.

The Captain stares out the window of the wheelhouse. I know his orders...heard them on Petersen's radio. "...*if* they are salvageable." And it's like I'm inside his head, and I can follow him. "These prisoners are baboons. Their stay on the island, cut off from all outside civilized contact, has rendered them hopelessly insane—they are beyond drug rehabilitation, an embarrassment to the United Nations Prison program. There is no question of attempting to round them up or herding them into the ship."

He's got to give the alternative order. Burn them off.

We can see it all. Wu Fang is now in a bamboo deck chair, behaving as if he's at a dull movie. I'm watching Margo as U.N. soldiers mass on deck, this time holding flame-throwers, grenade launchers. Then a row of fireturtles rumbles up behind them. I've seen them before, but I'm sure nobody in New Jerusalem has. They're baby tanks, curved backs like armadillos, flame nozzles on all four sides. The latest thing.

Margo's face changes, as the wonderful innocence brought her by the ship's first appearance fades horribly in a moment. She begins to realize what is about to happen.

One rifleman detaches himself from the group about to march off the ship. He moves to the steel railing of the liner overlooking the pier, glances up at the wheelhouse. The signal is given. He sights down the barrel, fires. On the pier, Big Tiny leaps toward the heavens, and at the top of his leap the little speck of steel lodges deep in his throat. He lands and his knees buckle as a thin stream of blood runs down his neck and wets his chest. He coughs, and pitches forward on his face.

The Kamoro cultists turn and flee, head back toward the city. Somewhere overhead, Big Tiny's bird of paradise plummets down through the clouds, falling helpless toward the earth below. The steel gangplank extends itself once more from the side of the ship, hits the pier, and the first of the fireturtles rolls down onto the soil of New Jerusalem.

We are ignored, the Black Bastard looking pretty much like a floating hulk, adrift in the bay. It takes no more than an hour. The dull boom of buildings falling, distant chatter of machine guns, occasional people racing toward the shore, clothes and hair on fire. The Kamoro cult, the good citizens on their way to the pier with their battered suitcases, and those who never even heard the news that the ship was to arrive—all of them never had a chance.

A gray roof of smoke hangs over the island. The fireturtles roll back to the ship, their job finished. The city of New Jerusalem is burning, and the sky is red with it. I saw this three times—a building, burned out to a shell of ash, and then, still holding its shape, rising, drifting up lazily into the sunshine, a ghost of itself, to dissolve in the air. Little floating house, bridge, dome—there and gone. Or maybe I'm seeing things.

The sport of the gods is played out in New Jerusalem.

Now it has been swept away. The people lie burning in the rubble of the tiny world they built, the dregs of someone's dream they turned into a model of their memories and twisting desires. Their tree of suffering has been hacked down, and now they sleep.

The last of the troops and fireturtles rumble up the gangplank. It is withdrawn smoothly into the ship's side. The U.N. Transport's foghorn sends out a triple blast, calling back to itself any of its stray servants. None come. All on board. The island is smoking. Dim hum of the ship's engines as it begins to back away from the pier. Job's over.

And that is how, through error and misunderstanding, the shameful, lustful, prideful, hopeful, confused, lonely, wise, foolish, guilty, and unrepentant citizens of New Jerusalem paid at last for their crimes. The Captain was right. They lived their lives like monkeys trying to grab the moon. They were not fit to return. Maybe I'm no longer fit to return.

Wu lights his silver pipe, turns a page in the book of the philosoper. He looks up at Margo and me.

"Today all the words seem to be there only to stop children from crying. A story." Wu Fang pauses a moment. "Go ashore. The canoe is at the stern. I will wait here for a while, to see if you return...."

Walking like firedancers through the glowing coals of the city of New Jerusalem, Margo looking like a pale angel, her step very light, and no tears come to her eyes.

It is all a burning, and a blizzard of ash, and then in my mind a sudden cooling snow comes to these ruins, landing to sizzle on the hot metal, a snowflake dissolves into the core of a blackened beam.

The rubble of Cowboy Dreamland, the house at number one Phoenix Road where Margo was born, Luck and Virtue Temple, the Octopus Lounge. Nothing remains. The burned body of Zuzu the pygmy lies in the doorway of Koon Wah Lithographers, her baby carriage a charred mass of melted aluminum.

The door of the Rock Bottom Academy, with its painting of a green boulder, still stands somehow. The rest of the building is ash. The body of the master, in his ceremonial robes, lies in the middle of what once was Change Alley. Around him are twenty dead United Nations soldiers, young boy faces, necks broken, backs broken, one with a tiny silver knife in his chest, a throw that pierced a bullet proof vest.

Corpses of whores, died with sunglasses and fur stoles on, heading for the ship, their cardboard suitcases black and charred. Faces of the dead that let you know that for them, even this won't turn out to be a real vacation. . . .

Phoenix Road, burnt out. Arnheim Quay, burnt out. Arnheim Boulevard, burnt out. A dog pokes his head around a corner, tongue dripping saliva that sizzles on a hot timber. A violet streetlamp flickers on, burns out in a flash and a thin stream of smoke issues toward the sky. Great flakes of thin gray ash fly upward and revolve over the ruins like drab and jerky pinwheels, swooping and diving, then rise toward the sun in a pillar of air.

Margo calls out that she hears something, and we are quiet
for a moment, and I hear it too. It sounds like a cat in pain,
or a child crying. We turn the corner, a small storefront, still
partly standing, that once sold faded postcards of New
Jerusalem in its glory. We go in. The fat proprietor is dead
behind his counter. What was once a kamoro on his
forehead is a smear of black plastic imbedded in what's left
of his face. His pet parrot is turned to burnt meat in a cage.
The crying is high-pitched, broken. Louder now. Then it
stops.

At the back, a trapdoor to a cellar. I go down. It's like
entering a steamroom, heat up far too high...hard to see in
the little light from the open trap. The room is a cellar dug
out of the earth, its walls and floor are black soil, burning to
the touch. Huddled in one corner is a tiny bundle of rags,
arms like stringy sticks, and eyes all white. It is the Kephi-
boy. His mouth is clenched shut in a grimace of pain, and
yet out of it comes a faint moan, as if from far away. He must
have been hidden away here by the cult, to wait out the
apocalypse, and then take the credit or blame on his tiny
soul. The underground room saved him from the flames.

I carry him up into the light and his whole body winces
with pain. He can't walk. I set him on the ground next to
Margo and he crumples, curls into a ball. Margo kneels,
cradles his ugly head in her arms. He blinks his eyes,
straining, stares up at her.

I stand. Even the air seems quiet now. Everything is
somehow distinctly clear, as if ten suns were shining. I look
out toward the harbor. The sail is slowly rising on Wu
Fang's ship. Then the black triangle reaches the top of the
mast.

Wu Fang sails slowly toward the mouth of the harbor, out toward the open sea. I don't imagine he expected our company. I watch him go. Margo stands, sees the Black Bastard moving away. She looks at me. The Kephi-boy is on his knees, hanging on to her leg, and making tiny sounds in his throat. We will have to find food for him. This black ash—plow it under. New Jerusalem is gonna be a garden.

The bay is empty, as if no ships had ever been there. The island is ours. Like anywhere else. Earth is our place. We live here and labor in its crust. We pay our way, but we're always looking for a good thing. If you've got it, then nurture it, protect it like people traveling in the wilderness protect their guide, as a one-eyed man protects his remaining eye, as ordinary people protect their children.

If you don't got it, come back yesterday. Come tomorrow, when the corn is green. We'll get lonely waiting for you. Here in New Jerusalem, we'll wait for you, a long time.

Trouble in paradise. Read about it in a good book. This one. *The History of New Jerusalem and How I Lived There*, by Faber the reporter. Your reporter. Here we are, all three. No doubt, my editor is expecting me. I have my story to write. He'll never see it. I hear voices saying goodbye. The party's over. Long time no see and it's goodbye. No see you now out there. Goo' bye, goo' bye. Now to work here. That's the last shot you see, back to the camera. My back to your camera. Now you just stand there, Mister Man, and watch us walk away. People of New Jerusalem walk away. City square, fading light, stink of burning, neon flickers by a window. I am there with my back to your camera, dark suit and dust rising. Someone is walking away.